A CHRISTMAS WALTZ

Merry was dancing with a young man she had met a few days earlier; unfortunately, he fancied himself a ladies' man, holding her altogether too close during the waltz. Before she could extricate herself from his warm embrace, she found herself looking into the icy eyes of Lord Barrisford, who ruthlessly cut in on them.

"You waltz well, sir," she said at last, when it appeared there would be no conversation at all, "but then I would have expected as much."

"You need to be more careful, Miss Melville," he said coldly. "Why did you allow that young man to hold you so closely? Don't you know that your reputation can be ruined in the twinkling of an eye?"

"If you were paying attention, Lord Barrisford," she returned, "I believe you will have noticed that I tried to disengage myself, but he would not let me go."

At the end of the dance, he informed her that they would be returning home. She offered no argument, but once in the privacy of their carriage, she let him know her feelings. "Why, sir, may I ask, did you think it necessary to drag me from the ball before I was ready to leave?" she asked.

"I think it should be obvious, Miss Melville," he responded coolly.

"I'm afraid that it isn't at all obvious to me, Lord Barrisford. Do explain it for me."

"Very well," he responded. "You were not being circumspect in your behavior. I would imagine that my grandmother, being old, has indulged you too much and allowed you to run wild."

"To run wild?" gasped Meredith indignantly. "Are you mad?"

For a moment Barrisford could not trust himself to reply. Then, suddenly so intensely aware of her presence next to him that he could scarcely bear it, he turned and swept her into his arms. He expected her to resist, but to his amazed delight, Meredith seemed to melt in his arms . . .

Books by Mona Gedney

A LADY OF FORTUNE
THE EASTER CHARADE
A VALENTINE'S DAY GAMBIT
A CHRISTMAS BETROTHAL
A SCANDALOUS CHARADE
A DANGEROUS AFFAIR
A LADY OF QUALITY
A DANGEROUS ARRANGEMENT
MERRY'S CHRISTMAS

Published by Zebra Books

MERRY'S CHRISTMAS

Mona Gedney

Zebra Books
Kensington Publishing Corp.
http://www.zebrabooks.com

ZEBRA BOOKS are published by

Kensington Publishing Corp.
850 Third Avenue
New York, NY 10022

Copyright © 1998 by Mona Gedney

Zebra and the Z logo Reg. U.S. Pat. & TM Off.

First Printing: December, 1998
10 9 8 7 6 5 4 3 2 1

Printed in the United States of America

One

"I *do* wish that Thea wouldn't fancy herself in love with every presentable young man that she meets," remarked Meredith, watching her younger sister anxiously from the library window.

Anthea, her dark eyes glowing, was being helped from the carriage by a young footman whose worshipful gaze was far too obvious. As she stood beside the young man, she allowed her hand to remain on his arm a few moments more than necessary, smiling up at him through lashes that looked too thick to be real.

"What's the minx up to now?" inquired her brother, hurrying to the window beside Meredith to take in the scene below them.

"Damnation! A footman!" His gaze darkened and he stalked toward the door, all six feet of his slender frame quivering with indignation. "You would think that if she *must* throw herself at someone, she could at least pick someone suitable! I'll go down and put the fear of God into her once and for all!"

"You'll do no such thing, Evan!" exclaimed Meredith, hurrying after him. "You know that she can't bear to have you order her about when you're only a year older than she is. If you were to read her a lecture, very likely she would elope with him to-night."

"No doubt!" agreed Evan bitterly, sinking into a leather chair by the fire and rubbing his temples. "After all, she's already eloped with one of our gardeners and a postillion from The Golden Boar. Why should she hedge at choosing a footman? And I suppose we should be grateful. After all, he really is more eligible than the other two."

"Good! Jenkins has seen her and is taking care of the matter," said Meredith with satisfaction, ignoring his complaints. The elderly butler had closed in upon the young pair, directing a glance at the footman that sent him hurrying indoors without a backward glance and shepherding Anthea toward the door. "I don't know what we would do without him. He found David for me this morning, too."

"Found David? I didn't know we had lost him," remarked Evan, momentarily diverted from his diatribe. "Had he run away again?"

Meredith nodded, turning away from the window. "It was after you had gone riding this morning. When Miss Riggs went in to awaken him for breakfast, she found a pillow under his covers. He hadn't been in bed all night."

Evan sighed. "He was a holy terror even before Father died—but I liked it better then. At least he was a cheerful little beggar. Why do you think he runs away at least twice a week, Merry? And I haven't heard him say three words since the funeral!"

She shook her head. David's behavior mystified her as well. Since their father's sudden death almost nine months ago, he had scarcely spoken to anyone, even when doing his lessons with Miss Riggs, and he had run away so many times that they could no longer keep count. Just where he was running they had not been able to determine, for he certainly wouldn't tell them and his direction was different each time. She thought that probably David himself had no notion of where he was going—except away from the pain.

Of all the children, James Melville's death had struck him the hardest. David was the youngest and the one who had been most attached to his father. All of the children had loved him, but David was the one most like him—and the one most in need of his company. Losing him just after Christmas last year appeared to have damaged David past repair. Meredith sighed as she thought what Christmas would be like this year. Surely it couldn't make her younger brother any more grief-stricken than he already was.

"Jenkins found him hiding in the loft of the stable this time. He hadn't even left the grounds." She turned back to the window, absently twisting the braided cord that held the curtains in place.

Evan turned to stare at her. "The stable? What on earth would take him out there? I haven't even been able to get him near the place since Father's accident."

James Melville had died within hours of being thrown from his horse, and eleven-year-old David had refused to mount a horse from that time, although he had always been in the saddle before his father's death. Not even the sight of Wellington, his pony, being exercised by the smallest of the stable boys had caused David to weaken.

"Bessie had her litter in one of the stalls," responded his sister briefly, and Evan nodded in understanding. Bessie had been their father's favorite hunting dog, and David now spent more time in her company than he did in that of his sisters and brother.

"How many pups did she have?" he asked, resigned. "I suppose we must keep all of them."

Meredith nodded. "Eight, I believe. David has three of them in his room."

Evan groaned. "Don't let him turn the house into a bloody kennel, Merry. Wouldn't one be enough to keep him company indoors?"

"That's a small enough matter, Evan—why trouble him right now about how many pups he can keep inside?"

He nodded at her slowly, thinking over her words. "I suppose you're right. Maybe he'll want to stay at home instead of running away if he knows he must take care of them."

Meredith grinned at him. "How clever you are, Evan! That's exactly what I'm hoping he will think."

"Well, you could have said as much instead of getting me all worked up for nothing," he responded tartly. "It isn't as if we don't have enough other things to keep us up in the air. What with Father's estate in limbo, no guardian to be seen on the horizon, Thea carrying on like a kitchen maid, and David refusing to communicate like a normal human being, there's no peace to be had in this household!"

"You're right," said Merry contritely, not mentioning that he could have added his own escapades to the list. Evan had once again been sent home from his school in disgrace, this time after he and two other young men had been caught "gambling in low company" at a local pub.

Merry suspected that the headmaster might have recovered from their keeping questionable company and even from the gambling, but he had not recovered from the fact that the young gentlemen had taken one of his wigs and waistcoats and had regaled everyone in the taproom with their imitations of him. His dignity wounded beyond repair, he had sent the students home with grim predictions of criminal futures for all of them. Since that time Evan had been studying with the local rector, preparing for Oxford.

"When do you think we'll hear from Barrisford?" he demanded, blithely unaware of the fact that he had asked her the same question no fewer than four times that day alone. "He's taking the devil's own time about coming."

"Do watch your language, dear," responded Merry absently, seating herself at the desk to read over the cook's menu for the day. "I'm sure that we will hear from him soon. After all, there's no telling where they had to travel to find him."

"Well, he ought to stay at home!" announced Evan belligerently. "How can he expect to hear from people who need him?"

"I don't suppose he had any idea that we or anyone

else might be needing him. No one expected Father to die—and then poor Mr. Hetherington's death was so sudden, too—"

She broke off abruptly, leaning low over her list to mask the tears that still came when she least expected them. Evan looked up suspiciously, but she managed to conceal her brief lapse. She knew that the others expected her to be calm and cheerful, and to be less than that would upset their already precarious emotional state.

"I suppose you're right," grumbled her brother. "Still, what kind of a fellow must he be, to go gadding off to the ends of the earth without keeping his relatives posted as to his whereabouts?"

"Probably a very happy fellow," returned Merry wistfully. "I should imagine it's wonderful to be able to travel wherever he wishes and to be answerable to no one."

Evan hugged her abruptly, thinking for once of someone other than himself. "I'm sure you must think so, Merry. We've been millstones about your neck for forever. At least when Barrisford comes you will be able to relax a little and we shall do all our complaining to him."

"Best not tell him that," observed Anthea brightly from the doorway. "He's likely not to come at all if he thinks he's to be set upon by a pack of Friday-faced tattle-boxes."

"Or if he finds that he's got to prevent your semi-annual elopements, Thea dear," retorted Evan sharply. "If we have any luck, he'll discover as little as possible about us before he comes."

Merry chuckled. Although she had no wish to say so, she felt that Evan was quite accurate. She was certain that Lord Barrisford would be less than charmed by the news that he had inherited the dubious honor of guardianship of the Melville children.

Nor was she alone in that certainty. Jeremy Bailey quite agreed with her—and he was the one who had been delegated to break the happy news to his lordship, a gentleman never known for the sunniness of his disposition.

"Hellfire and damnation, man! Don't trouble me with your problems or I'll fling you out this window! Go home to England and tell your bloody master that I won't come! I'm not at his beck and call!"

Jeremy Bailey, small and dry and hardened to the ways of the quality—especially the ways of this particular member of it—was unshaken by this eruption, and regarded the man before him with a benevolent eye.

"I'll tell him, of course, Lord Barrisford." He paused a moment before playing his trump. "Have you any message you would like to send to your grandmother?"

Barrisford turned from the window of his villa overlooking the Aegean to glare at him, and the clerk was suddenly uncomfortably aware that the powerful gentleman before him could snap his neck as easily as he could snap a twig in two. To his relief, however, Barrisford suddenly threw back his head and laughed.

"Calling in the heavy artillery, are you, Bailey?" he

demanded, sitting down abruptly and pushing a chair toward his wary guest. "I might have known that she would have a hand in this, too."

Beatrice, Dowager Countess of Barrisford, was noted as a most formidable lady, one whose wishes it was dangerous to thwart. Her only grandson had seldom done so, not because he stood in awe of her, but because he was very fond of her, despite her autocratic ways. And, since she had seldom demanded something of him that he was unwilling to do, their wills had seldom come into conflict.

Bailey permitted himself a brief smile as he sat down. "So it seems, sir. I hope that you will forgive my presumptuousness."

Barrisford rubbed his chin ruefully. "I wouldn't really have tossed you out the window, you know," he added apologetically. "No matter what I said."

"If you had, sir, I am sure that you would have been sorry for it and would have come down to see to my injuries," replied Bailey. "You were always kind, even as a boy."

"What you mean, Bailey, is that I am always sorry after my fits of temper," amended Barrisford, grinning. "Do you remember when we first met?"

"Very clearly, sir. You threw me into the river for interrupting your afternoon of fishing. I had an inflammation of the lungs for two weeks, and you came every day to read to me."

Bailey, clerk to James Fletcher, the solicitor of the Dowager Countess of Barrisford, had come that long ago day as a messenger from both the countess and his employer. It had been brought to the attention of the countess that her wayward grandson had once again removed himself from Eton without permission. Certain that he had gone to Sutherland, their country home, in order to hunt and fish, she had ordered Fletcher to see to it that he returned to school and was properly reinstated. Fletcher, after considering what he knew of the headstrong boy, had decided to delegate the responsibility for carrying out those orders to someone younger and more expendable. Bailey had been dispatched in his place, only to be confronted by a halfling who was already head and shoulders taller than himself and two stone heavier.

"I should imagine that my reading to you was more in the nature of a punishment for you than a kindness, given my limited scholastic attainment at that point," said the earl in amusement, "but you did become acquainted with my disposition. In view of that, I am amazed, Bailey, that you allowed them once again to send you to me with a message that you knew I wouldn't wish to hear."

Bailey looked at him kindly. "I have never feared you, my lord—at least, not after I recovered from my near drowning. You promised me then that you would never lay a hand on me again—and I have never known you to go back on your word—even when hard pressed as you were just now."

"Then you have more confidence in my forbearance than I," returned his host grimly. "Now tell me about this ungodly mess that my father left me heir to."

Bailey nodded and turned to business immediately. "As you know, your father was a good friend of

Robert Melville—actually, of course, there were three of them—your father, Melville, and Richard Hetherington, who were close friends at Oxford. They all agreed that if anything happen to one of them, the other two would care for his family should there be any need. Your father died first, of course, but there was your grandmother to care for you. And then Hetherington died, but his son was already of age."

Here he paused to clear his throat. "Now Melville is dead, and he has no other family to care for his four underage children."

"What of young Hetherington?" demanded Lord Barrisford, determined not to let another escape the responsibility that he was trying to avoid. "What's his name—Ralph? Isn't it time for him to be setting up a family of his own?"

"Dead, my lord," answered Mr. Bailey, his expression appropriately sad.

"Dead? How can he be dead?" demanded Barrisford. "He's a young man!"

Bailey nodded. "Very young indeed. He died in a sailing accident just a few months ago. He was the only heir, so there has been a great to-do to determine what will happen with his estate."

Barrisford's shoulders slumped slightly. "So it all does come back to me," he observed grimly, ruffling his dark hair in irritation. "I really am the only one left."

Bailey nodded quietly. "I am afraid so, my lord."

After a few moments of silence, Barrisford chuckled dryly. "Well, Bailey, it appears that it has done me little good to avoid parson's mousetrap so that I

could live as I please and go where I please, answerable to no one. I seem to be as neatly caught as
though some clever young miss, anxious to be a
countess herself, had led me to the altar."

"So it would seem, my lord," agreed Bailey, watching his charge somewhat anxiously. He knew his man
very well indeed, and he feared that his bitterness
did not augur well for the future.

Barrisford was notorious for his inability—and his
lack of inclination—to settle down and produce an
heir. Many a young girl had sighed for him—or for
his title and fortune—only to be ignored. From the
time he was a youth, his tastes had run to older ladies,
safely married, and to high fliers who had no expec-
tation of marriage. Having successfully avoided marriage and family, despite the encouragement of his
grandmother, he had always been free to rove as he
was now, sailing idly among the Greek isles or to India
or wherever else he pleased, answerable to no one for
his actions.

Bailey feared—with some justification—that he was
quite determined, despite the present imbroglio, to
keep things just that way.

"How old are the Melville children, Bailey?" he
demanded suddenly, eyeing the solicitor suspiciously.
"There are no babes in arms, are there?"

"No, no, my lord," Bailey was able to assure him
comfortably. "No such thing. The youngest one is
nine and the eldest is seventeen."

"And is the seventeen-year-old male or female?"
Barrisford inquired warily.

"A young lady, my lord," returned Bailey disapprovingly. To his way of thinking, there were proper and improper ways to speak of ladies. "Female" was not one of the words he used to refer to that gender.

Barrisford groaned. "That's all I needed to hear, Bailey! I won't come home to England to have some simpering miss hanging on my coatsleeve at every turn. I have spent my life avoiding just such horrors!"

Bailey had a sudden mental picture of the business-like Meredith Melville, who had efficiently run both the household and the estate during the past months since her father's death, clinging to Barrisford's coat-sleeve and allowed himself a dry grin.

"What are you smiling about, Bailey?" asked Barrisford suspiciously. "Did I say something to amuse you?"

"I was simply trying to imagine Miss Melville hanging upon your coatsleeve, my lord. I'm afraid that I simply could not picture it."

"You don't think that she would be interested in me? Is that what you're trying to tell me, Bailey?" Barrisford, although not really a vain man, was too keenly aware of his own value as a match to believe such a thing.

Bailey allowed himself a short, dry shrug. "I cannot imagine it, sir," he returned frankly. "She is a young lady with responsibilities and with much to occupy her mind. She has been caring for the rest of the family since her father's death several months ago— and she appears to be managing better than most adults would in her place—particularly given the difficulty of her charges."

Barrisford growled at him, slightly ashamed of his

earlier remark—but still suspicious. Years of exposure to young ladies hunting for husbands had made him extraordinarily cautious.

"I suppose that I must go home then," he growled ungraciously. "I don't want the fates of four hapless children weighing upon my conscience. It has quite enough to contend with already."

"I daresay, Lord Barrisford," agreed Bailey, allowing himself a brief, disapproving cough. It had not escaped his attention that Barrisford had pursued pleasure in a most shameless manner for the past years since his departure from London.

"Would you like for me to be more specific, Bailey?" inquired Barrisford in amusement, noting the disapproval and raising his eyebrow. "I would be happy to."

"Not at all, sir, not at all," responded Bailey hurriedly, ignoring his tormentor's grin. "I believe that we had best spend our time going over the details of Melville's estate."

To his dismay, however, Barrisford suddenly appeared to give consideration to his earlier lapse in prudence. When he had somewhat thoughtlessly mentioned the difficulty of Miss Melville's charges, he had hoped that his slip had been overlooked.

The earl looked at him thoughtfully, rubbing one hand through his hair. "When you said that Miss Melville's charges were difficult, Bailey, just what did you mean?"

Bailey permitted himself a small, dry smile. "Nothing that a man of the world—such as yourself, my lord—could not handle," he said confidently, ignor-

ing Barrisford's suspicious expression and hastily
turning the conversation back to the business affairs
of the Melville estate.

Two

And so it was that three weeks later, Devlin Carlton, the fifth earl of Barrisford, arrived reluctantly at the gates of Merton Park, the Melville home, prepared to assume—in name at least—the role of guardian. Jeremy Bailey had not accompanied him, for Barrisford was quite determined to handle affairs in his own way, and he suspected—quite rightly—that Mr. Bailey might be inclined to disagree with his approach. He intended to set their affairs in order in double-quick time and to appoint someone suitable—perhaps an elderly relative or, if necessary, a stable, older person that he would employ—to live with them on the estate. He, naturally enough, had no intention of remaining longer than was absolutely necessary.

"Well, Jeffries, it's a fair enough prospect, don't you think?" he inquired of his valet as they gazed out over the green park and the smooth expanse of lake. The sweeping drive, partially lined with tall hedges, arced down to the attractive manor house of white stone. "If we must spend a quiet week or two in the country, this might not be a bad place to do it."

Jeffries, who had not welcomed the return to England, presumed upon his long association with his master and responded with an injured sniff. His sense of propriety had already been deeply offended by being forced to ride in Barrisford's curricle rather than following behind him in a coach, safeguarding his trunks of clothing. When he had discovered that no such coach was being sent and that his master was not even planning on taking his valet with him, Jeffries had been duly horrified. Only great determination and Barrisford's fondness for him had won him a cramped position in the curricle with only a carpetbag to watch over.

Barrisford regarded him seriously for a moment, then turned back to the scene before them. "You are quite right, Jeffries. I shall stay one week to straighten out their affairs—a fortnight at the longest. Perhaps I shouldn't have come at all, regardless of any family obligation."

He considered the matter for a moment, then shrugged. "Well, no matter. We shall know soon enough." And they set off at a brisk clip down the drive.

As they sailed along between the hedgerows, a rock suddenly whistled past Barrisford's ear.

"The devil!" he exclaimed, glancing sharply over his shoulder to see if he could tell who had thrown it. He had no doubt that it had come from above—one of the neighborhood urchins in a nearby tree, no doubt. He straightened his shoulders and frowned. He would put a stop to such intrusions in pretty short order. It was clear that things at Merton

Park were not as neatly handled by the admirable Miss Melville as Bailey had thought.

When they swept up to the entrance of Merton Park, the door opened and an elderly butler made his dignified way down the steps, flanked by two stalwart footmen. As Barrisford leapt lightly down, his attention was caught by a young man who quite literally burst through the doorway, exclaiming, "By Jove! What a bang-up pair, my lord! I have never seen anything like them!"

Accepting this ardent tribute as no more than their due, Lord Barrisford smiled and bowed to the speaker. "I am glad that you approve, Mr. Melville."

He paused a moment. "I do have the pleasure of addressing Mr. Evan Melville, do I not?" he inquired.

Evan flushed to the roots of his artfully arranged dark locks. "I beg your pardon, my lord," he stammered, stepping forward to offer his hand. "It's just that I've not seen such a perfectly matched pair before."

Lord Barrisford smiled and regarded with satisfaction the pair of blacks he had just purchased at Tattersall's upon his return to London. "They are handsome, are they not?" he asked complacently.

"They are prime goers, my lord," breathed Evan reverently. "A bang-up set-out of blood and bone."

Barrisford nodded, pleased that at least one of his charges had impeccable taste and an appropriate attitude toward his guardian. This might all be easier than he had imagined it.

Just then a vision of feminine beauty issued from the doorway. The temptress was small and dimpled, dark-haired and quite delectable. Her liquid eyes met his and he was, for an unwary moment, transfixed.

"Lord Barrisford," said the vision in a throaty voice that promised everything, "How wonderful it is that you have come to us." And she floated down the steps toward him, one creamy arm outstretched.

As he bent over her hand, thinking that Bailey had made far too much of the businesslike Miss Melville, he heard quite a different voice—one in which there was no music and a considerable amount of ice.

"Lord Barrisford, this is Anthea, our younger sister. Forgive us for being so rag-mannered in our welcome."

The mood broken, Lord Barrisford looked up sharply at the speaker, a slender young woman with thick auburn hair that glowed in the sunlight. She also extended her hand to him, but he could feel her reluctance. As a matter of principle—and to annoy this chilly young woman—he bent over it and pressed it to his lips.

"And you must be the businesslike Miss Melville, I have no doubt."

Evan chortled. "The 'businesslike Miss Melville'— that's just what you are, Merry. He has described you precisely."

Meredith regarded their guest coolly. "Thank you for the accolade, Lord Barrisford. We shall see if I deserve it."

She paused and looked at the other two. "This is Evan and I see that you have met our sister Anthea— our *fifteen-year-old* sister," she re-emphasized sternly, for she had not missed the exchange between the two and she knew something of Barrisford's reputation.

Barrisford flushed slightly, annoyed to realize that he had almost overstepped his bounds with a school-room miss and been called to book by the presumptuous chit before him.

"And I understand, Miss Melville," he replied smoothly, "that you are only seventeen yourself."

"Not at all, sir," she responded quickly. "I turned eighteen just last Friday."

He bowed. "My abject apologies, ma'am. I see that I am dealing with a lady of advanced years."

Anthea smiled dewily at this sally and Evan hooted irreverently. "He's got you there, Merry! You are forever acting as though you are decades older than the rest of us!"

Having hoped to shake her composure slightly and to at least elicit a retort, Barrisford noticed regretfully that Miss Melville's lips merely tightened slightly, but she gave no other sign of her feelings.

"You must be tired after your journey," she said quietly. "Please come in and Jenkins will show you to your chamber."

He followed without speaking, somewhat shamed by her composure and by the fact that he appeared to have joined forces with two children. Still, it annoyed him that she seemed to take so much upon herself, and that she seemed so little impressed by him—quite unlike the beautiful younger sister, who clearly thought him all that a man should be. That was the way he was accustomed to being regarded. Certainly he could not recall encountering any female—particularly a young one—who had not found him captivating.

That Miss Melville thought him somewhat less than perfection became all too apparent to him in extremely short order. When they gathered for dinner that evening, Anthea was meltingly attentive to him, and Evan seemed equally disposed to hang on his every word.

"I trust, Lord Barrisford, that you are comfortable in your chamber," said Meredith, turning the conversation from tales of his travels.

"I am, Miss Melville. Thank you for inquiring," he returned.

"I am glad to hear it," she said quietly. "I had thought of giving you Father's chamber, but that seemed to upset David so much that I decided not to do so. If you would wish it, however, we could make that change for you."

Barrisford looked at her in surprise. "No indeed, Miss Melville. Why should I be taking your father's chamber rather than one of the guest chambers?"

"His is larger, of course, with an adjoining dressing room and sitting room. I was afraid that your present chamber would not be adequate after all of your luggage arrives."

"All of my luggage?" he asked, startled.

She nodded. "I know that you had to come quickly, but once all of your things arrive I believe that you will need more space. We do wish for you to be comfortable, of course. After all, it is five years until Evan is twenty-one and can take partial responsibility for us and another four until you are altogether free of us."

Barrisford stared at her in dismay. He had not realized that they would actually expect him to take up residence with them. Surely they must know that he had a life of his own to live.

"Of course, Merry," remarked Evan, noting the earl's expression, "it may be that he would prefer that we live with him at Sutherland. It would be only natural that he would wish to be at his own home."

"Nonsense!" exclaimed Meredith decisively, earning herself a look of profound dislike from her guardian. "It is useless to uproot us, particularly Anthea and David. And who would look after Merton Park if we were not here?"

She turned to Barrisford. "Naturally you have a staff to look after Sutherland for you, my lord, and at any rate I believe that I have heard it said that you are seldom there. Is it not far more sensible for us to remain here than for you to have to arrange for someone to care for our home?"

"How could I disagree when you have presented the matter so clearly?" he returned drily. What a managing chit she is, he thought to himself, grateful that he would not be seeing much of her. "I'm sure that we will come to a suitable arrangement."

The two younger Melvilles nodded, confident that the matter was in competent hands, but their sister, he noted, watched him with a very skeptical eye. Ignoring her, he turned the conversation back to his travels and did not notice when she slipped quietly from the drawing room.

When she returned a few minutes later, she was wearing a worried frown.

"Thea, have you seen David?" she inquired abruptly. "He should have been down fifteen minutes ago, and he isn't in his room now."

In honor of Lord Barrisford's arrival, all of the family was attending dinner that evening, even those who properly belonged in the nursery—like David—or in the schoolroom—like Anthea.

Anthea, who had been listening, enthralled, to an account of Lord Barrisford's encounter with pirates in the Mediterranean, turned to her sister with a certain degree of annoyance.

"No, Merry. I haven't seen David since nuncheon. Doesn't Miss Riggs know where he is?" she asked, her delicate brows arched in disapproval of her sister's interruption.

"Does Riggs ever know where he is?" inquired Evan, his tone light—until encountering Merry's gaze. "Should I go to look for him?" he added hurriedly.

Merry paused for a moment, then shook her head reluctantly. "If David wants to be found, he will be," she returned. "It would do us no good to miss dinner in his behalf."

Evan smiled in relief. "You're always sensible, Merry," he said approvingly. "I could spend the rest of the night looking for the little beggar and come back to find that he's been sitting all this while in the attic while I scuttle about and miss my dinner."

"I'm not certain that it's sensible not to look for him," returned his sister, her brow wrinkled in concern. "I just hope that he hasn't run away again."

Lord Barrisford, who was about to inquire into her

last remark, was prevented from doing so by one of the footmen hurrying into the drawing room, announcing loudly and with a decided lack of polish, "Miss Melville, come quick, miss! There's a fire!"

Merry rose quickly and followed him to the door, with the others in her wake. When they reached the front entrance, the truth of his statement was all too obvious. Lord Barrisford's curricle, which had mysteriously reappeared from the stable where it had been quartered, was afire. A brigade of servants, directed by Jenkins, was pouring buckets of water over it and quickly reduced the flames to a smoldering, sodden mess.

Barrisford regarded the ruin of his newly purchased vehicle with disbelief. "How did it come to be here?" he demanded sharply of Jenkins. "And who set it ablaze?"

Merry stepped between them and spoke quite pointedly to her guest. "Jenkins has just put out the fire," she said, eyeing him firmly. "Perhaps, my lord, it would be better to commend him for doing so instead of questioning him as though he were a suspect. He has been with our family for forty years."

Angered by her interference—and by the knowledge that she was well within her rights to make such a remark to him—Barrisford colored deeply. He inclined his head stiffly, acknowledging her comment, and turned back to Jenkins, his tone calm. "Do you have any idea who might have done this, Jenkins?"

"*I* did it! Not Jenkins, you silly gudgeon!" called a voice from above them.

Caught by surprise, the group on the drive stared

toward the chimney pots high above them. There stood a young boy in a blue jacket, clinging to one of the chimneys on a steep angle of the roof and glaring down at them vengefully.

"That's right! I did it—and I'm glad! You might just as well turn around and go back to wherever you came from! You don't belong here!"

And the small figure released his hold on the chimney and scuttled over the angle of the roof and out of sight.

"The little beast!" exclaimed Evan furiously. "Imagine his doing such an outrageous thing! I'll drag him down here—"

As he started toward the door, his sister caught his arm. "Don't go after him, Evan. You know that you won't catch him and you'll very likely break your neck. We'll deal with him later."

Her color high, she turned back to the astonished Barrisford, saying stiffly, "We must apologize for David, my lord. I'm afraid that he's taken our father's death very hard—"

"And he goes about setting fire to things in order to make himself feel better?" inquired Barrisford, his eyebrows arched in disbelief. "I shall keep a pail of water beside my chamber door tonight in case he suddenly needs to feel better again. Are there other charming family idiosyncrasies that I should prepare myself for?"

Meredith's expression did not alter as she said in the same stiff voice of one enumerating the points of a lesson carefully learned, "Well, Lord Barrisford, if you must know, Evan is inclined to gamble, drink, and get himself sent home from school on a fairly regular basis, while Thea satisfies herself with eloping only semiannually with the least eligible male available. And David, as you see, is apparently an aspiring arsonist."

Barrisford stared at her, trying to choke back a sudden rush of laughter. It was the first genuine amusement he had felt since being ripped away from his old life, and it was being afforded him by this stiff young woman who was ignoring the outraged expressions of her brother and sister. Doubtless she had no idea that her comments were amusing—she probably had not a trace of humor herself.

"And you, Miss Melville," he managed to return in a suitably grave tone, "just what is *your* fatal weakness?"

Without skipping a beat, she replied briskly, "I, Lord Barrisford, as you have noticed and remarked upon, am a shrew. I must always be the one to order others about.

"Now, if you will excuse me," she added, starting toward the front door, "I will deal with David. Evan, you will see to it, please, that everyone is suitably seated at dinner. I will join you as soon as possible."

Quite as good as her word, Meredith reappeared at the dining table within a quarter of an hour, accompanied by a slight, dark-haired boy, his forehead still creased with anger. He slid into his place without a greeting and rapidly applied himself to his dinner.

"Lord Barrisford," said his sister, "this is David."

Before he could respond, she turned to the boy. "David, I am certain that you wish to apologize to our guest for setting fire to his curricle. Nod your head if you are sorry for what you did."

David shook his head violently, a dark fringe of hair almost covering his eyes.

"Well, honestly, David, whatever were you thinking about?" demanded Evan indignantly. "Lord Barrisford is here at considerable inconvenience to stay with us, and all you have done is destroy his property—and a prime curricle at that! You damn well better be sorry, or I'm going to know the reason why!"

"Thank you, Evan," said Meredith calmly as David bent his head over his plate. "You've handled that very neatly. I'm certain that David will now apologize immediately."

She turned to Lord Barrisford and favored him with a small forced smile. "As you see, my lord, David is not inclined to talk. He hasn't spoken in the nine months since Father's death—or at least he hadn't until he shouted at you from the rooftop tonight."

She paused a moment, staring at her younger brother, then continued, "That is certainly no excuse for his behavior, however. I have no notion what caused him to do such a thing, and I do apologize on his behalf for all of us. I shall expect you to replace it at our expense."

"That's very kind of you, Miss Melville," nodded Barrisford, studying David, who still kept his eyes on his plate. This was undoubtedly the culprit that had heaved the stone at him when he arrived, and now he had burnt his curricle to a crisp and addressed him as a "silly gudgeon." The boy had obviously been allowed to have the upper hand for too long and would profit from a firm male hand. "I believe, how-ever, that I would prefer that David pay for the dam-age himself."

To his amusement, Barrisford found himself look-ing into the startled eyes of all the Melvilles—includ-ing David.

"Nonsense," returned Meredith briskly. "A boy his age has no money of his own, sir, as I'm sure you know."

"Then David may work out his payment for the damage," returned Barrisford smoothly, continuing with his dinner as though he were saying nothing out of the ordinary.

"Whatever could David do that would be helpful to you?" asked Meredith, astonished.

Barrisford shrugged carelessly. "I'm sure I don't know, ma'am, but my valet can certainly think of something—and, of course, there are my horses to be cared for."

"Your horses?" gasped Evan. "Surely you would not trust such prime cattle to a boy!"

Barrisford could see from the corner of his eye that this comment had caught David's interest. He shrugged carelessly. "Probably not—I expect you are right. Such a young one shouldn't be trusted with horses like those."

Evan, oblivious to David's interest in the exchange, sighed in relief. "I'm glad to hear you say so, my lord. Why, I wouldn't think *myself* of attempting to care for them—although I had hoped that you would take me up in your curricle and perhaps allow me to hold the ribbons."

Barrisford, still watching the youngest Melville without appearing to do so, nodded. "There will be no problem with that. I will send Jeffries to town to purchase another curricle and we will be back in business in no time."

Here he turned deliberately to David, whose head was once more lowered over his plate. "And I will, sir, expect *absolutely nothing* to happen to this one," he said deliberately. "Do I make myself clear, David?"

To his relief—and to the amazement of the Melvilles—David gave the smallest and briefest of nods. No one could see anything but the top of his head—but everyone understood that he had agreed.

The rest of the dinner was an unqualified success. In their collective relief, Meredith was almost pleasant and Barrisford was almost kindly—while Evan and Thea, each of whom had a private agenda—encouraged conversation about the outings they could take once the new curricle arrived. Evan pictured himself rounding the trickiest of curves with casual control, while Anthea imagined herself seated beside Lord Barrisford, who regarded her with ardent tenderness whenever he could look away from the road.

Lord Barrisford was as good as his word. The efficient Jeffries journeyed back to town the very next morning, charged with replacing the damaged curricle.

His master was left with duties of his own to execute. The Melvilles' solicitor was suffering from a severe case of the grippe and would not be able to meet with him until later, but Barrisford spent the better part of the next two days closeted with their bailiff and—to his dismay—with Miss Melville herself.

The two gentlemen were ensconced in the library, going over what seemed to Barrisford to be an avalanche of bills and titles and deeds, when the door opened and Meredith briskly entered the room, still dressed in her riding habit and pulling off her gloves.

"Good morning, gentlemen," she said, nodding her thanks to Jack Humphreys, the bailiff, as he rose to hold her chair for her. "I'm sorry to be late, but there was a problem at the Walters' farm. Their oldest boy was injured and they sent for me early this morning."

The bailiff smiled as he noted Lord Barrisford's raised eyebrows and startled expression. "As you see, Lord Barrisford, Miss Melville is quite indispensable to the neighborhood."

"But why should they send for you?" inquired Barrisford, puzzled.

"Their family has farmed on our land for eighty years. Why would they not send here for help?" she replied.

"She is being modest," responded Humphreys. "A good many of the families that live on Melville land rely on her good offices. She is very capable in the stillroom and the herbal remedies she learned from her mother are sought after—even by those living farther afield."

Barrisford looked at her curiously. "And so what did you do for the injured boy, Miss Melville?"

She looked at him seriously. "In truth, there was very little I could do. He had taken a bad fall, and his father wanted me to set his broken arm, but I sent for a surgeon so that I am certain it will be done properly. All that I could do was clean his cuts and give his mother a salve to put on them—and some herbs to brew a tea to ease the pain."

"And who will pay for the surgeon?" inquired Barrisford.

Her eyes met his directly. "We will," she said firmly, as though certain he would question the decision. "It was my decision, and heaven knows the crops are poor enough this fall. The Walters never have much, but they have always been good tenants."

"I see," murmured Barrisford. "However, Miss Melville, if you always choose to ride about the countryside playing Lady Bountiful, you will play ducks and drakes with your father's fortune, you know."

Meredith did not flush at his words—if anything, she grew paler. "I am not a simpleton, Lord Barrisford, and I am not playing at anything. I do no more than my father taught me to do, and I do not throw money away with both hands, as you appear to think."

"You certainly do not," agreed Humphreys. "She keeps the books for the estate, my lord, and she is accurate to the last farthing. In fact, Miss Melville knows as much as I do about the affairs of the estate, my lord. Her father depended on her after his eyesight got poor, and she took to it quite naturally.

"So I see," said Barrisford. So Jeremy Bailey had been right; she was indeed the "businesslike Miss Melville." And she certainly showed no interest in clinging to his arm—nor apparently to anyone else's, for that matter. "If my advice is not needed—

as it clearly is not—just what is my role? To sign the checks?"

Humphreys chuckled. "Well, to be sure, we do need for you to do that, Lord Barrisford."

On the whole, the meeting was not particularly satisfactory. He did not wish to be needed, for that might keep him here longer than he had planned, but it was profoundly annoying that Miss Melville was so self-sufficient. It would not have surprised him had she informed him that his presence at Merton Park was not even necessary. He wished to leave, of course, but it would be satisfying if she expressed her gratitude for the great trouble he had taken in coming here to help them.

Unbidden, his conversation with Jeremy Bailey came to mind. "Miss Melville has been carrying far too heavy a load for one so young," Bailey had told him. "With the responsibility of the estate and the younger children, she has had little enough time for herself."

Well, he planned to do something about that, although doubtless the peerless Miss Melville would not appreciate his efforts. Careful questioning had revealed that the Melvilles apparently had no other relatives that they knew of, so he had decided that making discreet inquiries for an appropriate older couple through his own solicitor—and not that of his grandmother—would be the best line of attack. God only knew how many highly respectable families had elderly relatives who were in need of funds. He would be providing a service both to the Melvilles and to the unknown—but doubtless grateful—couple. Then he would be free again—except, perhaps, for semiannual trips to London to sign whatever paperwork was necessary.

Satisfied with his decision, he strolled through the garden that afternoon, attempting to clear his mind of the annoyances of the day. Hearing a low murmur from behind a low brick wall, he approached it quietly and looked over it. David was leaning back against it, the three puppies he had adopted cuddled in his arms. Just what he was saying to them, Barrisford could not quite catch, but the boy's low crooning reminded him that this was a very lonely child, a child without enough to do—and a child that had deliberately destroyed his curricle and owed him payment for it.

He backed up quietly and then approached the wall, humming briskly. The crooning ceased immediately, and David stood up without the three pups in hand.

Barrisford started as though surprised by the boy's sudden appearance. "Just the person I've been looking for," he announced cheerfully. "Come along with me to the stable, and we'll get you started on paying for the curricle."

Involuntarily, David looked down at the puppies nestled at his feet. Noting his glance, Barrisford walked up to the wall and peered over it.

"Pups!" he exclaimed. "Nothing better! They can go down to the stable with us."

David scooped them up and trudged along behind Barrisford to the stable.

"See here, Toby!" Barrisford exclaimed as they entered its cool dimness. "I've brought David down to learn how to care for my blacks! Can you teach him?"

Toby, one of the older stablehands, emerged from one of the stalls. "O'course I can, my lord. No one better." Looking down at the pups, he said, "Best go put those back with Bess, lad. It'll be time for their dinner soon."

David nodded a reluctant agreement and trotted off to the farthest stall to return the pups to their mother's cozy nest. Barrisford remained long enough to be certain that Toby was indeed competent and that David was attending to his lesson, then sought refuge from the Melville family in the library, comforting himself with thoughts of blue seas and freedom and admiring women.

After an absence of three days, Jeffries returned with a handsome curricle. It was, if possible, an even more elegant equipage than the first.

"Don't let it out of your sight," Barrisford instructed Toby, handing him a guinea. "If you can keep it intact until I leave, I will give you ten of these."

"Yes, my lord," returned Toby blissfully, seeing his future secured by such a windfall. "The boy will not come next or nigh it."

The curricle proved itself to be the answer to several dreams. Barrisford took himself away from the household with regularity, satisfying his own deep need for a certain degree of freedom as he wove through high-hedged, narrow lanes. To his delight, Evan found himself with the ribbons in hand, being guided down the lane by an expert hand so that he learned to take a sharp curve as lightly and tightly as possible. Not to be outdone, Anthea, tricked out in her most becoming walking dress and bonnet, demanded a turn in the curricle and was driven out through those same country lanes, bowing elegantly to the few startled countryfolk they met along the way—and to three young gentlemen with whom she had danced at the last local ball. Happily for all concerned, David showed no immediate inclination to set this curricle afire and had allowed himself to be instructed so that he could properly care for the blacks.

"I must confess, Lord Barrisford, that I am amazed that David would do such a thing," said Meredith. It was a week after his disastrous arrival, and the two of them stood in the door of the stable, watching David meticulously currying one of the blacks under the judicious eye of one of the stablehands. "I never would have believed that he would take this kind of interest in horses again."

"He and his brother have a good eye for horses. David knew that these were particularly fine," he responded. "Your father must have taught them well."

She nodded, her expression softening for a moment as she remembered. She was quite taking, he found himself thinking, when she was not so cold and commanding.

"He did—and David was losing all of that." She paused a moment, then added stiffly, "Thank you, Lord Barrisford. Even though he still isn't talking, this seems like nothing short of a miracle to us."

Barrisford nodded, allowing himself the briefest of smiles. This was more the attitude he expected from those about him. His satisfaction, however, was short-lived.

"About time you said as much, Merry," announced the graceless Evan, whose approach neither of them had noted. "I suppose this shows you that he isn't the arrogant ass you said he was."

Realizing his error as he glanced at Meredith's horrified expression, he colored fiercely and tried to cover his blunder. "Of course, she didn't mean to say such a thing, sir. I'm sure that—"

"You know very well that I did mean it at the time I said it, Evan—and so does Lord Barrisford," responded his sister grimly "We won't insult his intelligence by saying otherwise."

Meredith straightened her shoulders as though forcing herself to face an unpleasant duty and added, "And I can see that I must have been wrong when I thought that you would take no real interest in our problems. I appear to have misjudged you, Lord Barrisford. I hope that you will accept my apology."

Hiding his amusement, Barrisford afforded her a brief, understanding bow, attempting to ignore both Evan's worshipful expression and her own more speculative one. It was clear that she was by no means certain that he deserved the apology. He knew very well which of the two had the more accurate estimate of his character, although it chaffed him severely to acknowledge it. After all, he told himself reasonably, what claim did they really have on him? And why should a red-haired chit of a girl make him feel so uneasy?

Three

To Barrisford's dismay and the delight of Anthea and Evan, an invitation to a neighborhood ball arrived the next day.

"I am certain that I am not included in the invitation," he demurred at breakfast the next morning after Meredith had read it aloud.

"Of course you're included, sir!" responded Evan, shocked. "Mrs. Anderson would never dream of leaving you out. After all," he added, grinning, "I daresay you're the drawing card for the whole event. Half the countryside will be there just to look at such a famous whip. I've told everyone about you."

"However can I thank you, Evan?" he responded dryly, trying to suppress a shudder as he considered the delights of a rural ball with a gaggle of Evan's friends clutching his coattails at every turn. "I am afraid, however, that I have business in London that will take me away for a few days."

Evan's face fell, but Anthea was still caught up in the thought of the ball and had no time to devote to Barrisford's defection.

"May I have a new gown, Merry?" she inquired, her dark, dewy gaze fixed upon her sister.

"I'm afraid that you shouldn't attend this affair, Thea," replied Meredith reluctantly, knowing that she was about to begin a row. "You know that you're not supposed to go to such events until you're officially out. We had enough trouble when you convinced Evan to take you to the Compton ball last month while I was ill. It wasn't suitable—as several of the ladies of the neighborhood have been by to tell me—and it won't be any more suitable now. I'm sure that Mrs. Anderson wasn't thinking of having you come."

"Only because no one would want to dance with her darling Janie if I were there!" replied Anthea pettishly, rising from the table, an unbecomingly mulish expression on her face. "Why must you always be such a spoilsport, Merry? What does it matter if I go?"

"As I have been trying to explain to you, what people think of you does matter, Thea," returned her sister patiently. "We must be especially careful of your reputation, not only because of the Compton ball but because—" Here she paused for a moment, trying to think of a delicate way to refer to the two attempted elopements so that she would not further aggravate the situation.

"Because you choose to run off with anything in pants that makes sheep's eyes at you," finished Evan brutally. "Why not say it straight out, Merry?"

He turned to glare at Anthea. "It isn't our fault that you've chosen to make yourself the talk of the countryside, Thea. Why, no man with the sense God gave a goose would consider making you an offer.

For all he knows you would run off with the first gypsy that came to the door selling hair ribbons."

Anthea trembled with scarlet fury and, snatching up her cup of tea, flung its contents at her brother before running from the room.

Unfortunately, however, she missed her target. Lord Barrisford, who was seated next to Evan, found his immaculate cravat suddenly sodden. Using his napkin, he wiped his face carefully and stared down at his valet's handiwork ruefully.

"I shall have a difficult time explaining this to Jeffries," he murmured.

"Forgive her, sir," said Evan grimly. "The little cat sometimes has no more manners than a guttersnipe."

"Speaking of Thea in such a way cannot help the situation, Evan," returned Meredith sharply.

"Merry, you can't take her part in this—"

"I'm taking no one's part, Evan—except that of our guest. However, if you hadn't deliberately antagonized her, we might have avoided this inconvenience for him and embarrassment for us."

"Pray don't regard me," said Barrisford affably. "I am merely pleased to see that Bailey can be mistaken. He had informed me that the admirable Miss Melville handled all difficult problems in the neatest, most efficient manner possible. I am relieved to see that even such a paragon of excellence as yourself occasionally has trouble."

"I have never considered myself such a paragon, sir," she responded, her voice cold. "And, although I see that you are taking some sort of perverse pleasure in this household upset, I assure you that I take no joy in causing distress to my family."

One glance at her eyes told him that this was the truth, and he felt some compunction for baiting her. She was, after all, not much more than a child herself, and he reminded himself sharply that he was here to set their affairs in order so that she no longer had to bear the responsibility herself—and so that he could remove himself from this imbroglio with all possible haste.

He rose and bowed to her briefly. "My apologies, ma'am. I forgot myself for a moment. With your permission, I will speak with your sister when she is somewhat calmer and see if I can convince her to accept your decision—which is most certainly the correct one—with a little more grace."

"If you can do that, sir, then you are a magician," responded Meredith.

To her amazement, however, he was better than his word. Within an hour Anthea rejoined them, her expression angelic. It was not until two days later—after his departure for the brief trip to London, having promised faithfully to return in time for the ball—that Meredith discovered he had promised to bring Thea a phaeton of her own with a fine black horse to go with it.

"What could have possessed him?" demanded Evan indignantly of Meredith. "She is ham-handed, Merry. She won't possibly be able to control an animal of any spirit."

"I'm certain that Lord Barrisford can be trusted to choose a horse that is suitable for Thea," his sister responded slowly. "But why on earth would he present her with her own transportation for an elopement?"

Evan stared at her. "You're right, Merry," he said after considering the matter. "Possibly he didn't think of that."

"One would think him more alert than that," she mused, "but perhaps not. Perhaps he does not think that she will be endangering herself even though she has so little judgment and with the phaeton she will have such freedom of movement."

Much struck by this observation, Evan nodded his head. "And of course she can be trusted to do something outrageous—the little ninny! How could Lord Barrisford, so awake on every suit, overlook such a thing?"

Meredith shook her head, but a most unwelcome thought had suddenly taken possession of her. What if Barrisford had in truth been more taken by their sister than she had supposed? What if he saw this as the way to take advantage of Thea's vulnerability?

"Surely not," she told herself. "That cannot be so. A man of Lord Barrisford's standing—who is also our guardian—would not ruin an innocent girl." But a voice deep within her kept insisting that he might have no difficulty in doing so if the girl were fetching enough—and if she had already shown herself determined to bring about her own ruin on several other occasions. And he had, after all, already taken her out alone in his curricle. Meredith had told herself at the time that there was no harm in it—he was, after all, their guardian, and the drives were very brief—usually with Evan riding beside them to study

his idol's technique. And, of course, had she not allowed it, Thea would have driven them all mad. Still,
the gift of a phaeton seemed unforgivably careless.

Barrisford, in the meantime, was congratulating
himself upon his splendid notion. He knew that the
gift would do two things well: calm Thea and agitate
her sister. He could not have been more pleased with
the idea.

Once in London, he went directly to his grandmother's house. He hadn't seen her in almost two
years, and the Dowager looked him over sharply
when he entered.

"Well, how was it at Merton Park?" she demanded,
noting with some satisfaction that he looked a little
worn. To her way of thinking, Devlin had had his own
way for far too long a time, and she quite longed for
him to encounter some trouble and to have a real
relationship with someone—a relationship that he
couldn't control. When Melville had died, she had
looked upon the problem of guardianship as a god-
send.

"Hellish," he responded shortly, throwing himself
onto the sofa.

The Dowager chuckled. "I had heard that the children are a handful. Do they have Melville's looks?
He was a handsome young devil, flashing dark eyes
and thick, dark hair."

"They're well-looking enough," acknowledged the
earl. "The younger ones must look like him. The
youngest is a hell-born babe who thought at first that

I was in league with the devil; the other boy is a nice enough halfling, although he is overanxious to make a splash in the world; and the younger girl will elope with anyone who asks her."

The Dowager studied him. "What of the other girl?" she inquired.

Barrisford snorted. "She makes the others seem like sweethearts by comparison—and she thinks that she can order me around like she does everyone else at Merton Park."

"Does she indeed?" The Dowager's eyebrows rose in amusement. "She ordered you about? I should like to have seen that."

The earl stared at her suspiciously. "She didn't manage it, if that's what you mean, ma'am—although it wasn't for want of trying. The chit actually thought that I meant to live with them!"

"Well, you are their guardian, Devlin. It's not unnatural that she would suppose such a thing," responded his grandmother mildly. "I'm certain, however, that you clarified that point for her."

"I most certainly did," he answered in grim satisfaction. "I will do my duty by them, but I won't be called to order by some schoolroom miss."

"I don't believe that she is just that—a schoolroom miss, I mean," she explained. "It seems to me that I heard that Melville's oldest child took over the household after her mother died, and she continued in that way when her father fell ill. Then, of course, he had the riding accident, and she was left completely in charge. I daresay she is accustomed to calling the tune."

Barrisford considered this. If Bailey had imparted this bit of information, he had missed it—which was likely, since his mind was otherwise occupied at the time.

The Dowager watched his face with satisfaction, then asked, "And what does the girl look like—is she dark like the others?"

"Meredith—Miss Melville—has auburn hair and blue eyes."

"She looks like her mother then," commented his grandmother. "Vivian Melville was accounted the beauty of the Season the year she came out."

"There's nothing amiss with her looks," he conceded reluctantly, unwilling to acknowledge that she was indeed quite lovely, "but her manners are far from taking. Why, the girl told her brother that I am an arrogant ass!"

"Did she indeed?" inquired the Dowager with a chuckle. "How sorry I am that I wasn't present."

"Her personality is abrasive," he responded defensively. "They call her 'Merry,' but nothing could be farther from the truth. There is nothing merry about her. Whoever marries her will live under the cat's paw."

After he had left, the Dowager spent an enjoyable evening before the fire, chuckling to herself over the troubles her care-for-nobody grandson was having. "I hope you lead him a merry chase, my girl," she murmured, lifting her glass of sherry to the absent Meredith. "It is more than time that someone did."

* * *

By the time Barrisford returned to Merton Park, Meredith had steeled herself to confront him and forbid him to present Thea with his gift. She had little doubt how such a man as Barrisford would receive such a demand, but she was certain that she had to protect her thoughtless sister.

So it was that Jeffries had scarcely made his master comfortable in the library after his return when Meredith appeared. She had commissioned Evan to drive Thea into the village to shop and take tea before returning home, so that she could deal with the problem privately.

"And did you bring the phaeton back from London with you, my lord?" she asked abruptly.

His eyes met hers in a level gaze, putting out his cigar since a gentleman never smoked in the presence of a lady. "I had a very pleasant journey, Miss Melville. Thank you for inquiring."

"You must forgive my lack of manners, sir. I'm afraid that I don't have time for them just now. Would you answer my question, please?"

Barrisford leaned back comfortably in his chair, his dark eyes gleaming with wicked delight. "I suppose, Miss Melville, that you fear your sister will use the phaeton to career about the country and get herself into even more mischief than she already does."

"I don't fear it, Lord Barrisford—I know it to be true. She is too young and headstrong to be given such free rein."

"And what makes you think she would have free rein?" he demanded.

Meredith stared at him. "Why would she not?" she

asked slowly. "She doesn't like to ride, but there's absolutely nothing to prevent her from doing as she pleases when she has her phaeton."

Lord Barrisford smiled. "You are overlooking her guardian—and yours, Miss Melville," he reminded her gently.

"But you're the one that has gotten it for her!" Meredith exclaimed in irritation. "If there is something that you should explain to me, sir, I wish that you would do so plainly so that I may understand you. Why will she not do as she pleases with the phaeton now that you have bought it for her?"

He stood and executed a brief bow. "Plainly, ma'am, I am forbidding Miss Anthea to take out the phaeton unless she has my express permission to do so."

Meredith stared at him blankly for a moment. "You think that Thea will obey you?" she demanded, her eyebrows lifted in disbelief. "And what is to prevent her from taking it out no matter what you say?"

"None of the stablehands will harness the horse for her—"

"Thea needs no one to do that for her!" Meredith interrupted, her brows knit with irritation. "She is perfectly capable of doing that herself."

"But she will scarcely be able to do so if the phaeton is in a shed, the shed is padlocked, and the key is in my pocket, Miss Melville. I would have told you this had you given me a chance to finish what I was saying."

Meredith sat down abruptly. "So you never planned for her to be running wild in the neighborhood?" she asked. "I must apologize, Lord Barrisford, I'm afraid that I thought—"

"That I would allow a silly young widgeon with more hair than wit to gallivant about the countryside, making a byword of herself and her family," he finished affably.

She nodded.

"And you thought, perhaps, that I felt that allowing such behavior would reflect credit upon me?" he inquired gently.

"No, of course not, but—"

"But your dislike of me made you feel that I might not be clever enough to work that out?"

"Oh, you are clever enough, Lord Barrisford, but not, I'm afraid—" Here she stopped abruptly, for she had almost betrayed her fear that he might wish to encourage Anthea in such behavior for his own ends.

"Do you believe that I would countenance such behavior?" he demanded angrily. "Is that what you were about to say?"

She shook her head silently, fearful that if she said anything else, she would make a greater mess of things. Finally she murmured, "Thea can be quite captivating when she wishes, Lord Barrisford."

He stared at her in disbelief. "Do you think that I am interested in her?" he asked.

Meredith nodded wordlessly.

Ignoring the fact that he had at first glance found Thea very alluring, Barrisford seethed with righteous indignation, pacing up and down the length of the library as he attempted to control his anger. Meredith watched him with interest.

"I must confess, Lord Barrisford, that I had not

thought you would care so much about this—or, to be honest, about anything."

He stopped abruptly and stared down at her, his eyes as hot and piercing as his voice. "And that is your opinion of me, Miss Melville?" he demanded. "That I care about nothing at all?"

Meredith did not give way, although his physical presence was almost overpowering. He stood intimidatingly close and his was the advantage since he was staring down at her.

Folding her hands carefully in her lap, she gave herself a moment before meeting his eyes and replying. "It would appear to be so," she said simply. "I know that you have helped us, but I know too that you have done so because you feel it to be an obligation, not because you care about what happens to us."

Barrisford stared at her, startled to feel his fury mounting because of the truthfulness of her words and the calmness with which she made her observation.

Taking advantage of his silence, Meredith rose. "Now, if you will excuse me, sir, I have things to do before Thea and Evan return. We must be certain that there is a suitable place for the phaeton to be housed where it can be kept under lock and key as you have suggested."

Barrisford caught her elbow before she could move toward the door. "Do you never become angry or show your emotions, Miss Melville?" he demanded. "Do you not have any blood flowing in your veins?"

Meredith looked pointedly at his hand on her arm. "You forget yourself, sir."

"And perhaps you should forget yourself for a moment, ma'am," he returned, pulling her toward him.

Ignoring her angry protest, he pressed her to him and kissed her fiercely, enjoying the sensation of power as she struggled against him. After a few moments, Meredith recognized the uselessness of her struggle and forced herself to relax and to yield to his kiss.

Congratulating himself upon gentling her, he released her enough to be able to move back a few inches and was amused to see her first reach up to smooth her hair into place and then behind her, apparently to straighten her sash. What he failed to note until too late, however, was that she was actually picking up a China vase, which she proceeded to break across the top of his head. Taken by surprise, he released her and pressed his hand to the cut on his forehead that was already beginning to bleed.

"You were right, Miss Melville," he managed to call before she reached the door.

She turned to look back at him and he smiled and bowed. "You are indeed a shrew."

"And you, sir, are indeed the arrogant ass I thought you." She paused before leaving the room. "Press the palm of your hand to the cut and try not to bleed upon the sofa cushions or the rug. I will send Jenkins to you directly."

And the door snapped smartly closed behind her.

Four

"What do you mean, 'He fell,' Merry?" demanded Evan, dogging his sister's footsteps as she inspected a row of vials in her stillroom. "A man like Barrisford doesn't fall into furniture—unless of course he is three parts disguised, which he wasn't. What the devil happened? Jenkins said he had a gash the size of—"

"Evan, do stop being so tiresome. Go away and find something to occupy yourself until dinner." Meredith had no intention of telling anyone how the accident had occurred. Jenkins had used sticking plaster to cover the cut and Jeffries had hurried his master away to be certain that the job had been properly done.

"And what am I supposed to do?" he asked plaintively. "I've spent the afternoon with Thea as you asked—and had a perfect horror of a time I might add. And now that I've come home, I find that Barrisford has been bleeding all over the library and is now bleeding in the privacy of his chamber, you have retired to your herbs and elixirs, and Thea is demanding to know where her phaeton is. I suppose by now she is already halfway across the countryside in it, probably with that footman she's been making eyes at."

"No, she isn't," responded his sister complacently.

"How can you be so sure, Merry?" he asked, suddenly curious. "And why aren't you out there to be certain that she isn't?"

Merry patted her pocket. "Because the phaeton is locked away and I have the key."

Evan whistled. "There won't be any need for a fire in the house when Thea finds that out. She'll provide all the heat we need."

The truth of his observation was demonstrated almost instantly. The door of the stillroom was flung open and Thea entered it like a whirlwind, her curls in tumbled disarray and a dark smudge on the pink skirt of her muslin frock.

"Where is it, Merry?" she demanded. "Where's my phaeton? None of the stablehands will tell me. Toby just stood there like a brick wall when I told him I'd have his job if he didn't show me where it is!"

"Have his job?" interrupted Evan indignantly. "Who are you to be telling him such a thing?"

"I'll do it, too!" said Thea defiantly. "He's no right to keep my own possession from me! Lord Barrisford would fire him if I asked him to!"

"Lord Barrisford would do no such thing," a suave voice assured her. Its owner lounged in the doorway, watching the group before him with amusement.

"And why would you not?" Thea pouted. "You told me that my happiness was your primary concern and that was why you were bringing me the phaeton."

Meredith cast him a glance that spoke volumes—

none of them pleasant—and Barrisford cursed himself for saying something that could be so misinterpreted.

"Of course your happiness is a matter of concern for me," he replied smoothly. "After all, I am your guardian." He glanced at Meredith to note the effect of his words, but encountered an expression that he was beginning to know well: her eyebrows were raised and a small, knowing smile barely curved the corners of her lips. She didn't believe a word he was saying.

"Then where is the phaeton you promised me?" she demanded. "I don't like empty promises."

"Don't you?" retorted Evan. "Then why on earth did you run off with that fool who promised to take you to Barbados and swore that he loved you? He disappeared soon enough when we paid him off."

Thea flushed darkly, and Merry, anxious to protect the contents of her stillroom, said hurriedly, "Let's finish our talk in the drawing room, Thea, and then we'll have one of the stableboys bring your phaeton to the front drive so that you can see it."

"So they *do* know where it is!" Thea said triumphantly. "I thought as much!"

"Well, they do know, dear, but they can't get to it themselves," explained Meredith, ignoring Barrisford's suddenly interested expression. "I have the key to where it's kept."

"The key!" exclaimed Thea. "Why must it be kept under lock and key?"

"And why, Miss Melville, do *you* have the key?" inquired Lord Barrisford.

"You were . . . indisposed, sir, and so I took the

liberty of making the appropriate arrangements for the phaeton," she responded pleasantly, ringing for Jenkins. The elderly butler appeared promptly, casting an interested look at Barrisford's forehead as he accepted the key from Meredith and listened to her instructions.

"The devil!" murmured Barrisford, encountering Jenkins' glance and turning toward the fire. He rested his hand on the mantel and shoved impatiently at a protruding log with his boot. He detested highhanded young women and he was certain that he had detected a gleam of amusement in the butler's glance.

"What happened to your forehead, Lord Barrisford?" inquired Thea, able to take an interest in other matters now that she had had her way. "Are you well enough to drive out in the phaeton with me?"

"Yes, of course I'm well enough," he replied brusquely, ignoring her first question.

"But what happened to—" she began again, but before she could finish, Jenkins came hurrying into the room, moving with undignified haste.

"Miss Melville, Master David has taken the phaeton!"

"Taken the phaeton?" repeated Meredith blankly. "How could that be, Jenkins, when it was locked up?"

"He took the hasp off the door, miss. The padlock is still locked."

Lord Barrisford's laughter rang through the room. "I congratulate you, Miss Melville! You have done a very thorough job of securing the phaeton!"

"I did precisely what you said you were going to do, Lord Barrisford!" she reminded him sharply.

"But I would have taken greater care and perhaps anticipated such a thing had I been the one to do the securing!"

"You, sir, were too busy bleeding to think of such a thing. If you had—"

"Excuse me, Miss Melville," said Jenkins, finally managing to break into this interesting exchange, "but there's more. Master David took Lord Barrisford's blacks to pull the phaeton."

"What!" exclaimed Evan in outrage, starting for the door. "Why, he's likely to damage them! The little fool!"

The others hurried after him, and Meredith and Thea watched as the two men swung into the saddles of their horses. Toby had brought them up as soon as he had seen David riding out and sent a message up to the house.

It was twilight when they returned, Lord Barrisford grimly driving the phaeton, with Evan riding beside him, leading his mount, and David huddled next to him in the carriage.

"Whatever possessed you to do such a thing, David? Are you all right?" asked Meredith anxiously as she hurried toward them.

"You'd be better served to ask if the horses are all right, Merry," said Evan, with a touch of asperity.

"Oh, no!" she exclaimed, looking first at the pair of blacks and then at Lord Barrisford. "Have they been injured?"

He shook his head.

"But no thanks to David that they weren't," said Evan. "The little fool ought to know better than to take out horses he can't handle."

"Actually, he was doing quite well with them," remarked Lord Barrisford unexpectedly. "And I've been wondering, David," he continued, turning to look at the boy, "just why you took the phaeton when my curricle—the one you *didn't* burn up—has been available all this while."

This thought had been nagging him during the course of the chase, and he was quite sure that he knew the answer. There was a silence, as though they all thought David might speak, and then Barrisford went on to reply to his own question.

"It's because you knew you could handle the four-wheeled phaeton, isn't it? You were afraid that you'd take a spill in the curricle and hurt the blacks."

David looked up at him a moment, a sudden glimmer of warmth in his dark eyes. Then he dropped his head again, but he nodded.

"Nonsense!" snapped Evan. "He no more thought about that than a roast goose can fly! He just took it because he wanted to."

"I don't think so, Evan," returned Barrisford quietly, still watching David's bowed head. "I think that he knew just what he was doing and that—even though it was wrong of him to take the blacks without permission—he wanted to take good care of them."

The boy's dark eyes glanced up swiftly once more and then returned to studying the toes of his boots.

Meredith watched the exchange with interest. David wasn't accustomed to having a champion, and she wondered what the result of that would be. And how unlike Barrisford to go out of his way for anyone when he had nothing to gain. But, of course, she thought hurriedly, keeping his horses in good order was certainly vital to him. Probably the exchange with David meant no more than that—another self-serving gesture of kindness.

"Well, if it's quite all right with everyone, I'm going to go for a drive now in *my* phaeton. After all, if I'm not to be allowed to go the Andersons' ball, I must have some amusement."

Thea looked coyly at Barrisford from beneath her dark fringe of lashes. "Will you come with me, my lord?" she asked, certain of his response.

Mindful of his unpleasant interview with Meredith that afternoon, Barrisford answered briskly, "I'm a little tired, Thea, and it's getting dark, so the ride will have to be brief. Why not have Evan drive you?"

"Evan!" shrieked Thea. "My brother?"

Evan too looked anything but gratified, but when she announced that she would be holding the ribbons, he shook his head.

"I'm not getting up in that thing with you, Thea, unless I'm driving. I'm not about to go jauntering about in the dark with you falling into every pothole and breaking the axle on the first evening you own it."

"Very well," Anthea pouted, relinquishing the reins to her brother, "but tomorrow in the daylight I'm going to drive so that everyone may see me."

"However, Thea," said Lord Barrisford, "you will need to get permission from me before going—and

I will also have the key. Rest assured that it will once again be under lock and key."

Evan drove briskly away before Thea could reply, which was probably a wise move. Meredith turned to Barrisford.

"So you think that you can make a better job of locking it up than I did?" she inquired.

He nodded affably. "I'm certain of it, dear lady. It merely takes a little common sense to work this out satisfactorily." And with this thrust he smiled and turned to walk into the house.

"I look forward to seeing just how you handle matters, sir," she called after him. Just before he reached the door to enter the house, she called out again. "And don't be worried about the cut, Lord Barrisford. I daresay it won't be disfiguring—but if there appears to be a problem, I do have a salve that could work wonders on it. Or perhaps you could say that it was the result of a duel."

He didn't dignify that with a reply, but instead went inside, closing the door quietly. To his irritation, behind him he could still hear the sound of her laughter.

Five

Barrisford was very much upon his dignity when he came down to breakfast the following morning. Much to his surprise, however, he found a cheerful company at the table, with even Meredith assuming a pleasant manner.

"I'm so glad that you got back from London in time to go the ball tonight, sir," said Evan brightly. "You wouldn't believe the number of people who are anxious to make your acquaintance."

Barrisford groaned inwardly, for he had forgotten all about the ball. The events after his return home yesterday afternoon had kept his mind fully occupied.

"I still think it's a shame that I don't get to go, too." Thea appeared to be about to embark upon her list of grievances when Meredith, with a skill born of long experience, interfered swiftly.

"I expect that you will be too exhausted to do anything tonight, dear," she observed.

"Why?" asked Thea, momentarily diverted.

"You are taking your phaeton out today, are you not?" she asked briskly.

Thea brightened for a moment then, remembering

Barrisford's stricture from the night before, glanced at him and said sulkily, "I'm sure that *I* wouldn't know whether I may do so or not."

Meredith, foreseeing a day of recriminations and tantrums if he refused, looked at Lord Barrisford almost pleadingly.

Recognizing her look of desperation, Barrisford decided that he would show her how badly she had misjudged him. "Of course you may, Thea," he returned pleasantly. "And, since it is such a lovely day, perhaps you and Evan could drive to the river for a picnic."

Seeing their horrified expressions, he added quickly, "I would be following in my curricle, of course."

At this, Thea's face grew sunny again, but Evan looked at him unhappily. "Wouldn't I be able to go with you, sir? Perhaps I might drive for a bit to show you how I'm coming along. I've been practicing, you know—in my imagination," he added hurriedly.

Considering this for a moment and thinking of how long the day would be with Evan in constant company, Barrisford unhesitatingly sacrificed Meredith. "I'm afraid that it's already going to be rather snug in the curricle, what with Miss Melville and David."

"Merry and David?" responded Evan in disbelief. "David won't want to go with us. He never does."

Lord Barrisford turned to David, who had been eating steadily throughout this exchange. "What about it, David? Wouldn't you like to go—and perhaps hold the ribbons for a bit?"

David nodded briefly as Evan stared at him in horror.

"Surely you don't mean that, sir!" he exclaimed. "David couldn't possibly hold them and keep the curricle upright. The blacks would certainly be hurt—to say nothing of you and Merry!" he added as an afterthought.

"It's kind of you to include us in your concern, Evan," Barrisford replied drily, "but I assure you that I will not let David do anything that will endanger any of us."

He paused a moment, glancing at David, who was staring firmly at his plate. "And I must say that he seems a natural with horses. I don't believe I know many men with his touch."

To Meredith's amazement, David looked up for just a moment and smiled. Not even with the pups—which he still carried around with him—did he smile.

She stared at Lord Barrisford in wonder—such a selfish man, and yet he seemed to know exactly what David needed.

"And what about you, Miss Melville?" he asked, giving her a challenging glance. "Will you accompany us?"

Just moments before she had vowed to herself that nothing short of a miracle would convince her to take her place beside him in that curricle. And who had been expecting a miracle?

"Of course I will, Lord Barrisford," she replied calmly, raising her cup of chocolate to her lips. "I wouldn't dream of missing such an excursion."

They got underway far more quickly than Meredith

would have thought possible. The cook, possibly grateful that she now wouldn't have to serve any more meals that day except for a late supper for David and Thea, bustled about the kitchen, putting together a picnic nuncheon in record time. Thea, who normally required an hour to change her dress, was ready in half that time, and no one had to be sent to find David. He was standing beside the curricle when it was time to go.

The three of them in the curricle was indeed a snug fit, so it was fortunate that David was small for his age. During the times that Barrisford allowed him to take the ribbons, he placed the boy firmly in front of him and guided him carefully. Meredith was amazed by how seriously David watched everything that Barrisford did, and Barrisford spoke to him always as though they were having a conversation and he expected the boy to answer him.

They reached their destination with no more mishap than Thea driving the phaeton into a ditch. Fortunately it was shallow and there was no standing water in it—only a little mud. Nonetheless, by the time Evan had gotten out and led the horse back onto the road, tempers were frayed and neither of them was speaking to the other by the time they spread the cloth for the picnic.

"You did very well, David," said Lord Barrisford, leaning back against a tree trunk and skipping a stone across the smooth surface of the river. David didn't reply, of course, but he smiled.

"And Thea, too, did wonderfully well," said Evan caustically, surveying the wreck of his jacket and his muddy boots. "I daresay everyone in the shire will be after her to drive them out into the country so that they too can destroy their wardrobes."

"Well, if Evan hadn't been so busy telling me just what to do and how to do it, I might have had more time to watch for the turns," snapped Thea, tossing back her dark curls. "And if I had been with a *gentleman,* he wouldn't have minded at all getting muddy to help me."

Evan snorted inelegantly, and attacked his cold partridge with more ferocity than necessary. "I swear, Thea," he said, forgetting that he was not speaking to her, "if you treat men the way you treated me today, you will end up an old maid and I shall have to take care of you the rest of my life."

"An old maid!" she exclaimed angrily. "There is absolutely no chance of my becoming one, Evan, as you very well know. Although just where you'll find a woman who is ninnyhammer enough to wed you, I'm sure I couldn't say! You'll be coming to my home as a bachelor uncle when you're old and gray."

"How nice that you could join us for this family outing," observed Meredith pleasantly to Barrisford. "I do hope that you're enjoying the fruits of your gift. I daresay this is just the beginning."

He grinned at her. "I suppose that should make me feel very low, Miss Melville. To be quite honest, I am enjoying the outing. You were very pleasant company in the curricle."

She stared at him with a puzzled frown. "But I didn't say anything at all, Lord Barrisford."

"Just so, ma'am, just so," he responded, grinning again. "How rare a thing that is for you."

Meredith stiffened. "I am no chatterbox, sir, if that is what you're trying to imply."

"Not at all, ma'am. It is merely that when you do speak, you speak as though no one should question you."

She considered that for a moment; then he noticed with misgiving that her eyebrows were arching and the slow smile was beginning. "In other words, Lord Barrisford, I behave just as you do—and you find that troubling."

"In an inexperienced young woman," he said defensively, "yes, I do. I think that a certain respect for authority and experience should be allowed."

Meredith laughed outright, controlling herself only with difficulty.

"And just what do you find so amusing about that, Miss Melville?" he demanded.

"There is nothing wrong with what you said, Lord Barrisford. It is merely that I am trying to picture you as a very young man, giving your respect to those with authority and experience." She laughed again. "I fear that is not a picture I am able to conjure up. You are simply accustomed to calling the tune and find it difficult when not everyone dances to it."

To his annoyance, she continued to laugh until it was necessary to wipe her eyes on one of the linen napkins.

"I don't see that it is as amusing as all that," he said a little stiffly, unused to being the subject of laughter.

"But it is," she assured him, wiping her eyes one final time. "If you could only see yourself, pokering up and looking for all the world like you were twice your age."

"Twice my age!" he exclaimed. No one had ever accused him of looking—or acting—old. He was, in fact, accustomed to think of himself as quite a dashing fellow.

The other three had been watching them silently, amazed by the exchange.

"I say, Merry, I don't think that you are showing Lord Barrisford the sort of respect he deserves," said Evan, finally deciding someone else must take a hand in the matter.

"Thank you for your support, Evan," said Barrisford gravely.

"Of course, sir. Do you think I might drive the curricle on the way back and let Merry ride with Thea?"

"By no means," Barrisford assured him. "I can see that it is absolutely necessary that you be present to help Thea should she need it."

Thea glared at him, but he grinned and pointed to Evan's boots. "Aside from which, those boots are not coming into my vehicle."

"Nor into mine," echoed Thea warningly. "You'd best clean them up, Evan, or you'll be walking home."

"And it is time to be turning toward home," Merry reminded them. "Remember that we have to have time to get ready for the ball." She had been uneasy about referring to the ball, fearful that Thea would once again grow moody, but she remained in good spirits.

As they gathered up and started toward the horses, Thea glanced at Lord Barrisford's forehead curiously.

"Just how *did* you get that cut, sir?" she asked.

He flushed a little and touched the sticking plaster self-consciously. "It's a long story," he said uneasily, unwilling to become a laughingstock by telling the truth.

"I'll just bet it is," returned Evan, glancing suspiciously at Merry's bland expression. "I'd like you to show me sometime just how you managed to fall in such a manner that the vase fell with such force onto your forehead."

Meredith said nothing, and there was no further reference to the matter until they were back in the curricle. David had chosen to ride in the phaeton, curling up to sleep on the backseat, so she and Barrisford were alone.

"I do have some salve that would help your cut, Lord Barrisford," she said helpfully.

"I don't need it," he assured her. "I am doing very well as things stand."

She glanced at the cut. "I don't think so," she responded. "The skin is beginning to pucker at the edge of the plaster. You're likely to end up with quite a scar if you don't take some precautions."

"Well, as you so kindly noted, Miss Melville, I can always tell everyone that I got it in a duel and I will soon become a figure of romance."

She shrugged. "Very well, sir. If that's what you wish."

"Of course that's not what I wish! I don't want the

scar!" he exclaimed in irritation. "Bring me the damned salve, then. It seems the least you can do after attacking me."

"Attacking *you?*" she returned, her voice rising. "How can you say such a thing to me after what you did?"

"Nothing so scandalous," he said defensively. "It was just a kiss."

"It was a kiss that you forced upon me, sir, taking advantage of your superior size and knowing full well that I did not want you to kiss me!"

"No?" he asked, grinning. "You didn't want me to kiss you?"

"You know very well that I did not."

"It seems to me that there was a moment when you were not quite so sure of that," he responded.

"I would point out, too, Lord Barrisford, that I am your ward. It does not seem to me to be in the best of taste to force yourself upon someone who is in no position to refuse you."

He was well aware that her point was a good one. He had thought of it himself—but only after he had given way to impulse and kissed her. After a moment he nodded silently. "Touché, Miss Melville," he said quietly. "You are quite accurate. I apologize for my boorish behavior."

She inclined her head slightly in his direction. "I accept your apology, sir—and I promise that I will take care of the scar for you."

"And will you perhaps save a dance for me tonight, ma'am?"

She smiled. "I believe that I have one left," she

murmured. "If so, sir, it is yours—although I fear that I should be staying at home tonight."

"Staying at home? Why should you do such a thing and miss the ball?"

She nodded toward Thea. "She will be home alone tonight, with only the servants and David to keep her company. I am worried that she will manage to get herself in trouble again.

"Nonsense!" he assured her. "The phaeton will be under lock and key and little Thea will be so exhausted by the events of the day that she will sleep like a baby."

"I hope so," said Merry reluctantly, "but she never does what you expect her to do."

"You are making too much of it," he assured her. "Tonight you may have a good time with a mind at ease."

Six

And, greatly to her surprise, Meredith did have a good time. A better time, in fact, than Lord Barrisford had planned for her to have. Or at least for different reasons than he had in mind.

Barrisford was somewhat startled to see that Meredith was in great demand as a partner. He at first thought that perhaps it was simply because she danced well—which she did—but he soon learned that it was more than that. As he watched her, he made a surprising discovery—she had a very playful nature. She laughed with the young men who were her partners and showed no sign of lecturing them in the manner of "the businesslike Miss Melville."

When finally his turn came to dance with her, he looked down at her questioningly.

"It appears that perhaps I do not really know you, Miss Melville," he commented.

Her eyebrows raised, she smiled. "And indeed how could you expect to, Lord Barrisford? You have been here less than two weeks—and part of that time you have been away. How do you get to know another person in so short a time?"

He smiled down at her, his expression more gentle than she had seen it before. "And once again you are right, ma'am. Is it your habit to be always right?"

She nodded. "A habit I try never to break, sir. But I know that it is a habit that you admire since it is your own as well."

"But I fear that I may not be *always* right. It has occurred to me that I may occasionally be guilty of an error in judgment."

"Do you have anything in particular in mind, Lord Barrisford?" she inquired, just as the movement of the dance separated them.

"Indeed I do, ma'am," he responded as he rejoined her. "I believe that if you think back to our last encounter in the library, you will understand me."

"I understand you very well," she replied, not meeting his eyes.

"Then I hope that you will accept my apology, Miss Melville. I am indeed sorrier than I can say that I was so indiscreet."

Meredith looked up at him, certain that this was another of his smooth and convenient ploys for getting his own way, but when her eyes caught his, she realized with a catch in her throat that he was, for once at least, sincere.

"Of course I accept your apology, sir," she said lightly. "How could I not when it is so graciously offered?"

"Fencing with me, Miss Melville?" he inquired affably, a warmth in his eyes that she had not seen there before. This was not the heated look he had had in the library, but a tender one. It was unfair that a man should be able to look so tender—it was disarming when she was most in need of remaining armed.

"How could I hope to hold my own against you, Lord Barrisford?" she inquired. "From the beginning I must acknowledge your far greater experience."

Before he could respond, the dance had ended and he led her back to their table, where she was promptly claimed by a callow young lad (or so thought Barrisford to himself) and returned once more to the dance floor.

"Perhaps we should go to the cardroom, sir," observed Evan, materializing suddenly at his side. "I understand that it is lively tonight and there are several of my friends that would like to meet you."

Barrisford shook his head and settled himself at the table. "You go ahead, Evan. I believe that I should stay and play propriety so that your sister does not forget herself."

"Merry? Forget herself?" he asked disbelievingly.

Barrisford nodded, never taking his eyes from Meredith. "One never knows how these young men will conduct themselves. It appears to me that I should be watchful."

Evan looked at him quizzically. "Does it indeed, sir?" he asked. "I was not aware that Merry had any difficulty remembering the appropriate way to behave."

Lord Barrisford was still carefully watching Meredith and her partner and missed the dryness of his inquiry.

"Yes, but I know from my own experience that it is best to keep an eye on things so that these young men

have no opportunity to take advantage of their partners."

Evan grinned to himself as he made his way to the
cardroom, thinking that perhaps it wasn't merely the
young men that needed to remember themselves. He
had begun to have a very fair idea of how Lord Barrisford had received his wound.

As Barrisford sat and watched Meredith dance,
fending off as best he could Evan's forays with young
friends to introduce and talk with, he saw that she
was even more taking than he had begun to think.
Her hair, which had first caught his attention upon
his arrival at Merton Park, glowed red-gold in the
candlelight, and her pale skin was warmed by the
glow. Dressed in a gown of old gold, she seemed to
be dressed in candlelight.

Suddenly he jerked himself to attention. She was
nothing but a girl—and his ward at that. He had been
too long away from his old life. It was shocking, he
thought, the way a mind could wander when kept
from its own proper setting.

Somewhat to Meredith's surprise, the ride home
was a rather quiet and cool one. Evan was occupied
with thoughts of the money he had lost and Barrisford was trying to decide the earliest date he could
make his departure from Merton Park and England—and Miss Melville. The quiet made the shock
of activity at home strike them even more powerfully
than it otherwise would have.

Jenkins met them on the drive, wringing his hands
in a most pathetic manner.

"Oh, Miss Melville, I am so sorry, miss. I don't know how it happened."

"How what happened, Jenkins?" she asked patiently, patting his hands to calm him.

"It's Miss Anthea. She's gone again—this time in her phaeton—and she's taken James with her."

"James?" said Merry blankly.

"The footman, Merry—that blasted footman!" exclaimed Evan viciously, leaping from the barouche and heading for the stable. "Well, I suppose we must go and find her. Heaven only knows where she's gone this time. With any luck we'll catch her quickly before too many people learn that she's eloped again."

"You may stay here, Evan," said Lord Barrisford brusquely, brushing by the boy. "I'll change to my riding gear and then I'll need my horse," he told Jenkins, taking the steps two at a time.

"But you'll need me, sir. I know some of the places she's likely to go—" He broke off when he saw that Barrisford was out of hearing. "Don't you think I should go, Merry?" he demanded, appealing to his sister.

"We must do as Lord Barrisford thinks best, Evan," she said calmly, cursing the phaeton silently with every breath she drew. At least now he would know that he must be more careful with Thea—if they could only find her so that they *could* be careful of her again. Meredith tried not to think in negative terms, but it was hard indeed not to let her imagination wander. Thea ruined, with no future to look forward to. Still, Lord Barrisford was a capable and determined man. She herself would not want him on her heels.

"But what can we do, Merry?" Evan asked plaintively. "We can't just sit here and wait."

"The first thing that I need for you to do, Evan," she said, recognizing his need for activity, "is to go upstairs and make certain that David is asleep in his bed."

Evan groaned. "Lord, yes! That's all we would need—to have both of them run away at the same time. At least there are two sane members of this family."

Sane? Meredith thought to herself. Perhaps—or perhaps not. She was no longer certain.

A few minutes later Evan rejoined her, an expression of satisfaction spread across his face. "He's still here," he announced. "In fact, he's sound asleep with all three pups in bed with him."

"Good," Merry murmured. At least one of them was taken care of. For a moment she felt certain that tears would overtake her. Why could they not get themselves together and live life properly? They seemed always to be making a fearful muddle of things, even when they tried their hardest to have things go well.

The two of them sat together in the library, drinking the coffee that Jenkins brought them and waiting for news. It was not, however, until shortly after dawn that the wanderers returned, a grim-faced Barrisford leading a rather shamefaced Thea. James the footman was nowhere in evidence—which was just as well since he most certainly would have come to harm at Evan's hands.

"Thea." Meredith rose and put her arms around her sister. It was proof, she thought, of how thoroughly exhausted and miserable Thea was that she accepted the embrace. "Come along with me and let's put you to bed."

She paused as they reached the door of the library and looked back at Barrisford, who was standing by the fire. "Thank you, my lord, for bringing her safely home."

He met her eyes somberly. "It is my fault, as you well know, Miss Melville, that they were able to escape so quickly. It seems that I must apologize once again."

"Nonsense," said Meredith lightly. "It isn't as though this is a problem that just began to occur. It has been going on for some time."

"I realize that—but that only compounds my sin. I knew that and yet I got her the phaeton, thinking that I would be able to control her so that an elopement would be less likely." He did not add that at the time he had given no thought to the fact that he would soon be departing and leaving them with the problem.

Meredith was silent, for he knew that she agreed with him, but was reluctant to rub it in.

Finally, however, she said, "Thea ran away simply because we had gone to the ball and she wished to be there, too. I'm sure that it would have happened even if you had not gotten her the phaeton. That just made it easier for her—it didn't give her the idea."

Lord Barrisford smiled ruefully. "I didn't expect

kindness from you of all people, Miss Melville. Be careful."

She looked at him, puzzled. "Careful? Of what?"

"Of kindness," he responded wearily. "I have discovered that kindness in women works as an aphrodisiac for most men."

She thought about her reaction to his sudden tenderness and laughed shortly. "Perhaps the same is true for women of tenderness in a man."

The following day was what even the cynical Barrisford described as idyllic. The weather itself had a glowing autumnal peace, people and landscape alike gilded by the rich gold of the season. Thea was reasonably calm and Evan less fretful than usual, while David paid them the rare compliment of his company.

As they sat in the garden for tea that afternoon, Barrisford was steeling himself to announce his departure. He had received a letter from his solicitor that morning, saying that he had found a suitable couple and they would be coming to Merton Park later in the week. He knew that soon he would have to tell the Melvilles about the arrangements he had made for them, but thus far there had been no real opportunity—or so he told himself.

He watched David and Meredith playing with the pups, and found himself again hypnotized by the burnished glow of her hair in the autumn sun. Least of all did he wish to tell her. Nonetheless, it had to be done.

"Miss Melville," said Jenkins, appearing suddenly at her side, "a Mr. and Mrs. Pagett are here with their

luggage. They say that they are expected." He looked
at her questioningly.

"Pagett?" she inquired. "No, we're not expecting
them, Jenkins. Perhaps they've gotten the wrong direction."

Jenkins shook his head. "No, miss. They were very
clear. It was Merton Park and they knew your name.
They knew Lord Barrisford's name, also," he added,
glancing toward him.

Barrisford had been paying little attention, being
more pleasurably occupied with admiring the high-
lights of Meredith's hair in the changing light of the
sun, but at Jenkins' words he came to life.

"Who is here?" he asked, suddenly apprehensive.

"A Mr. and Mrs. Gerald Pagett, my lord," responded
the butler.

Barrisford groaned and everyone looked at him
with concern.

"Whatever is the matter, sir?" asked Evan. "Are you
ill?"

"No, not ill—just negligent," he responded guiltily.
"Mr. and Mrs. Pagett are the couple that my solicitor
has employed to stay with you."

"To stay with us?" said Meredith blankly. "Why do
we need someone to stay with us?"

"Since I will be leaving soon—" he began, but he
was unable to finish his sentence.

"Leaving!" exclaimed Thea. "Where are you going?"

"To Sutherland?" asked Evan eagerly. "May I go
too, sir?"

"No, not to Sutherland," he responded. "I need

to visit my grandmother again and then—" Barrisford paused, unable to bring himself to say that he was going back to the Mediterranean.

"You're going to visit your grandmother again?" Evan repeated.

"Precisely," he agreed. "Which is exactly why the Pagetts are here. They will be on hand so that you have someone reliable to consult when problems arise."

"How long will you be gone, sir?" asked Evan. "Will you be back in time for Christmas?"

Barrisford began to grow restive. This was going worse than he had anticipated. Reluctantly he shook his head.

"You're not coming back, are you, Lord Barrisford?" inquired Meredith coolly. "You're leaving the country again."

He looked up at her to find her regarding him with the same speculative glance she had at first. Once again he had proved she could not trust him.

Barrisford nodded. "I am returning to Greece," he said, "but I will certainly write to you, the Pagetts will be here, and my solicitor will be available for any problems that arise."

"How very convenient for you," observed Meredith drily.

"Be realistic, Miss Melville!" he said impatiently. "You know very well that I cannot take up residence here. I have lived my own way for too long to give it up."

Turning from her, he started to speak to David, but the boy and his pups had disappeared. Disappointed,

Barrisford walked slowly from the garden to meet the new couple. He had wanted to tell all of the family, but especially Meredith and David, about his departure before the Pagetts arrived. He had certainly not intended to make such a muddle of things.

Despite the fact that Gerald Pagett and his wife were a likable enough pair, dinner was an abysmal failure. David remained in the schoolroom to eat, and Thea went to bed early with a headache. Meredith had virtually nothing to say and Evan could only repine over his lost opportunities to become a first-rate whip. It was with intense relief that Barrisford made his escape from the drawing room and went early to bed.

Breakfast the next morning was equally frosty, and Barrisford was congratulating himself on his imminent departure when Jenkins entered with a disturbed expression.

"Miss Melville, I am afraid that Master David is missing again," he announced.

"Has anyone seen him?" demanded Barrisford, rising abruptly. He knew that this instance of running away was his fault.

Jenkins nodded. "About dawn this morning one of the hands saw him sinking a pair of boots into Miller's Pond. He was filling them with rocks so that they would go straight to the bottom."

That would explain the disappearance of his new Hessians, Barrisford commented to himself wryly. Jeffries had been unable to find them this morning, and David had doubtless taken them to make a statement of how he felt about his guardian. Barrisford sighed.

The fault was certainly his. It looked as though the search would be his as well.

It was several hours before Barrisford was able to find David. He had checked to see if the pups were with their mother, and to his dismay, they were. Barrisford had been hoping that they weren't and that David would be returning them soon so that their mother could suckle them. Thwarted, he set out to Miller's Pond to try to trace the boy's steps from that point.

He could find no one else who had seen him, and after riding about aimlessly for an hour or two, suddenly thought about the roof of the manor. The boy had taken refuge there after burning the curricle; perhaps he had done the same after sending the boots to their watery grave.

And it was there that he discovered David, lying flat on his back beyond the ridgepole of one of the steeper rises. Barrisford, for all his courage, was not a man fond of heights, and he waved to the boy from his own less precarious position.

"David! Come down here! I need to talk to you!" he called.

David did not stir.

"David! I know that you can hear me! Come down here!"

There was still no sign of movement.

Barrisford sighed. "Very well," he called, making his way back toward the attic window he had crawled from. "I had thought that perhaps I wouldn't leave after all—but I can see that it doesn't make any difference to you. I might as well go."

As soon as the words were out of his mouth, Barrisford regretted them. He closed his eyes and cursed himself. What on earth had possessed him to say such a thing?

When he opened his eyes, David was making his way toward him across the ridgepole.

Barrisford sighed. What had he done?

Seven

He was still wondering that two days later as he once more approached London and his grandmother's home. He had been determined to see the Dowager after he had realized at the ball that his behavior with Miss Melville had been far other than it should have been—but he had also planned to leave England and temptation almost immediately thereafter. Now he would be returning.

After resettling David and promising him faithfully that he would be back at Merton Park within a week to stay at least until Christmas, he and Jeffries had made their departure.

"Madness, Jeffries—that's all it could be attributed to—a moment of sheer madness," he said as they drove down the drive to the Dowager's home. "But I couldn't leave that boy up on the roof, could I?"

Jeffries, who had begun to develop his own theory as to the reason for his master's peculiar behavior, said briefly, "I could have."

"No, you know very well that you could not have, Jeffries, despite your care-for-nobody attitude."

"He drowned your new boots in the pond,"

pointed out his valet, upon whom this outrage had been working for some time.

"Yes, but he was overwrought. He thought that he was being deserted again—first his father leaves him, then I do. It was understandable."

Jeffries shook his head. "Being upset is understandable. But taking someone else's boots—new ones made by Toby and polished with my own special champagne blacking? That's criminal, my lord, no two ways about it. There's no telling what he'll do next. First your curricle and then your boots. Next it could be one of us," he added darkly.

"Nonsense! David won't do anything else because I'm not going to do anything to give him reason to do so," said Barrisford firmly.

"Meaning you'll never leave Merton Park?" inquired his valet.

"No, of course I'll leave Merton Park—but I'll do it a little later—in a way that won't distress the boy."

"Have you decided what that way will be?" asked Jeffries pointedly.

"No, but I have confidence that it will come to me," said Barrisford with his customary air of assurance. "In the meantime, we'll just have to make the best of things, Jeffries."

Jeffries was of the opinion that his master was not as unhappy with this arrangement as he had at first indicated. The valet had resigned himself to spending the additional time at Merton Park, but his greatest fear was that, unlikely as it had at first seemed, Barrisford might wish to settle there permanently. Jeffries had assessed Thea's charms immediately and knew her to be no threat, but Miss Melville was quite a different matter—an unknown quantity, so to speak. Ever since she had clipped Barrisford with the vase, the valet had viewed her in a new light. His master was not accustomed to females that stood up to him, and Jeffries feared that this extra time would give that interesting relationship time to develop.

Barrisford too, after recovering from the initial shock of having committed himself to stay for three more months, began to think that there could be benefits from a longer stay. He and Miss Melville might be able, with time, to establish a better relationship—one more suited to a guardian and his ward—and he could show her that he was indeed a force to be reckoned with.

Certainly all of the Melvilles—including Meredith—were in need of guidance and a firm male hand, he thought complacently. No doubt this would all work out for the best. That was the pleasant thought that kept coming back to him, so he found himself able to face the three months with greater equanimity than he might have otherwise.

The Dowager was delighted to see him again.

"In need of a holiday already, Devlin? They must be wearing you to a thread."

"I am in need of your advice, ma'am," he said gravely, seating himself next to her on the sofa.

Caught off guard, she stared at him for a moment, satisfying herself that he was indeed serious.

"*You* are in need of advice, Devlin?" she asked, her astonishment evident. "I don't believe I've ever heard you say such a thing."

"I don't believe I've ever been in just this position before," he responded. "I'm afraid that my behavior with Miss Melville has been injudicious."

His grandmother blinked. He might possibly have asked for advice before, but she was certain that he had never before admitted that he had made a mistake.

"Just what was the nature of this—injudicious behavior?" she inquired.

Barrisford flushed uncomfortably. "I kissed her," he said briefly.

"And did she respond?"

He flushed even more darkly and pointed to the sticking plaster. Meredith had been quite correct. He had needed the ointment—and additional plaster.

"She *struck* you?" demanded the Dowager incredulously.

"She broke a vase over my head," admitted her grandson. "And she has since pointed out to me that my behavior was unsuitable because I forced myself upon her and doubly so because I was her guardian and should be protecting her."

The Dowager remained silent for a few moments, both because she was amazed and because she was afraid that if she tried to speak, she would begin to laugh and not be able to stop. A single look at her grandson's face told her the truth of the situation. Barrisford had perhaps finally met his match. She marshaled her thoughts quickly.

"You admit that what you did was wrong, Devlin, so what is it that you would ask of me?" she asked.

"I know that it is my responsibility to do something

about this situation with Miss Melville, but I'm not certain just what that should be," he responded.

"Once you're no longer there, the matter with Miss Melville won't be a problem. Since you will doubtless be leaving soon, is this really an issue you need to settle?" she inquired curiously.

He nodded. "I'll be there at least until Christmas. I have promised as much to the younger boy."

"I see," she murmured, pleased by the news. That gave her a fair amount of time to work. "I think, Devlin, that the wise thing would be to have her come here to me for a few weeks. The rest of you can come at Christmas to spend a few days here with us."

His face fell. "You think she should come here to London?"

The Dowager nodded briskly. "You need to have some time away from her and it's more than time that the child had an opportunity for a holiday. I know for a fact that she's never had a season in town. I'd have her come to me sooner, but I'm going to be out of town myself for two weeks. After that you can send her to me."

Two weeks should be enough for propinquity to work, she thought with satisfaction. If there were already sparks flying—and vases—after so little time, two weeks should serve to intensify the situation. Then she would have Miss Melville come and she would see to it that the child had a good time. She was quite certain that her grandson would not be delighted by the number of eligible young men that would be interested in Miss Melville. That should serve to fan the fire.

"And so you really think that I should send her here? She's only just turned eighteen, you know."

"Pshaw!" responded his grandmother. "You astound me, Barrisford. You know that this is the time for the marriage market. I was married by the time I was eighteen. Miss Melville merely needs to meet some people and to leave her responsibilities behind her. Who knows? I may very well be able to find her a husband."

Barrisford nodded a little unhappily. "I suppose you're right," he said slowly, "but—I'm afraid that her younger brother will miss her sorely."

To say nothing of you, added his grandmother inwardly, silently rejoicing. Miss Melville had accomplished more than the Dowager could have hoped for—and in a remarkably short time. She looked forward to meeting that young lady and to encouraging the match. It was high time that Barrisford settled down—and settled down with a wife of spirit who would not allow him to browbeat her.

Eight

Much to his surprise, Lord Barrisford discovered that it was pleasant to be welcomed home—even though, as he reminded himself quickly, Merton Park was very far from being his home. David was waiting for him on the front steps, having watched for the curricle from the rooftop as Evan later informed him. Evan and Thea both greeted him eagerly enough too, although Thea had an undoubted interest in being able to take her phaeton out now that he was home and Evan had designs on the curricle. Meredith's welcome, as he had expected, was much cooler, and she waited until that evening at dinner to greet him.

He also found the Melvilles' solicitor, now recovered from the grippe, awaiting him. Mr Dyer, a distinguished-looking, gray-haired gentleman, greeted him apologetically.

"I hope, Lord Barrisford, that my absence has not inconvenienced you too much," he said, as they settled themselves at a table in the library late on the afternoon of his arrival.

"Not at all, Mr. Dyer," Barrisford assured him.

"Humphreys and Miss Melville have been over much of the paperwork for the estate with me."

"And done an excellent job of it, I'm sure," he replied, beaming. "I am delighted that you are taking such an interest in everything."

"Well, it seems that I do need to be acquainted with matters here," said Barrisford. "I must admit that assuming responsibility for a family and their affairs is not what I had in mind for myself, but I do want to be certain that I handle affairs competently."

"Very admirable, sir," Mr. Dyer commended him. "I realize that this is all very different from the life that you have been used to."

Here he hesitated a moment, then continued somewhat reluctantly. "I have met Mr. and Mrs. Pagett, Lord Barrisford, and Miss Melville explained to me why they are here. While I think that it is admirable that you have brought in substitutes—"

Barrisford held up his hand. "Actually, sir, there's been a change in my plans. I will be here through January, Mr. Dyer."

"And then?" the solicitor inquired.

"And then I will return to Greece."

"I see." Mr. Dyer seemed downcast, and Barrisford tried to rally him.

"You must not be fond of travel, sir," he said.

Dyer glanced up, a little puzzled by his comment. "Travel? Oh, but I am—indeed yes, I am very fond of it."

"From your expression, I had thought otherwise," Barrisford explained. "You look quite grim."

"I'm afraid that I feel quite grim, Lord Barrisford.

You see, sir," he responded slowly, "if you are unable to spend the majority of each year in residence with the family—at the place of your choice, of course—the guardianship of the Melvilles will have to be reassigned."

"Reassigned?" he demanded. "To whom?"

The solicitor nodded his head. "That is the question, of course."

"And—?" Lord Barrisford prompted him impatiently. "What is it that you are trying to say, sir?"

"That there is one very distant relative who could become their guardian should you not wish to take the responsibility," responded Mr. Dyer, polishing his pince-nez slowly.

"I thought that there were no relatives, Mr. Dyer," snapped Barrisford. "Do we have them coming out of the woodwork now that I have come forward?"

"Only one," returned the solicitor, "although the children know nothing of him. Indeed, I should imagine it was because of him that Robert Melville made the agreement with his two friends. Certainly no responsible man would wish Sir Gerald Crawley to be guardian of his children."

"Why not?" asked Barrisford with unseemly eagerness, suddenly realizing that he might have found his means of escape. "Has he committed heinous crimes? Has he been guilty of neglecting his family, for instance, since no one has heard of him?"

Mr. Dyer cast him a reproachful glance. "I think you might know that if he has been avoided, there is good reason for it. Robert Melville was a reasonable, just man and a good father."

Barrisford had the grace to look slightly shamed—but only slightly. Since Mr. Dyer's most unwelcome news about the terms of the guardianship, he had remembered Miss Melville's words about Evan's age—there were nine more years to go before he would be completely clear of the Melville brood. It suddenly seemed to him more than reasonable that a family member—like Sir Gerald Crawley, for instance—would have a greater obligation to the Melvilles than did he, a total stranger.

"My apologies, Mr. Dyer," he said more calmly. "Just what is it that Mr. Melville held against his relative?"

Mr. Dyer shook his head. "I don't actually know, my lord," he answered regretfully. "Mr. Melville never confided in me—more than likely because he did not think that it needed to be a matter of concern. It seemed, after all, very unlikely that his children would be in need of a guardian, or, if they were, that there would be any difficulty about one of his friends or their children fulfilling that need."

Barrisford sighed. More than likely, he thought, there was no greater problem than that Sir Gerald was an unknown factor—or perhaps that there had been some family falling-out generations back. He would have his own solicitor look into the matter.

"I daresay that Sir Gerald would not be interested in assuming the guardianship at any rate," Barrisford commented absently, seeing the next nine years of his life stretching before him like a prison sentence.

"Quite the contrary," returned Mr. Dyer drily. "He has already been in touch with my office, offering his services in any capacity they might be needed."

Barrisford brightened, seeing the door of his cell opening slightly. "That seems very goodhearted—quite a positive sign, I would think."

"A little too goodhearted," returned Mr. Dyer. "He said that he would be only too glad to take up residence at Merton Park and care for the children."

"You see?" demanded Barrisford. "What could speak better for him when we know that most men do not care for children—or at least for having to care for them?"

"Just so," agreed the solicitor, "but he also inquired about the ages of the young ladies and the amount of money that they had been left. Those did not strike me as disinterested questions"

Barrisford paused for a moment, then shook his head. "Perhaps we are being too quick to judge, Mr. Dyer," he said placatingly. "After all, perhaps Sir Gerald is merely anxious to know the details of the family situation."

"Perhaps," said Mr. Dyer, looking at him closely. "It will, naturally, be your decision, my lord."

"My decision?" asked Barrisford blankly. "What do you mean?"

"If you decide to stay with the Melvilles, you will be their guardian. If you do not, Sir Gerald will, by default, be appointed."

Barrisford sat back in his chair and studied the toes of his highly polished Hessians. (He had replaced the pair that had descended to the depths of the pond.) He acknowledged to himself that he did have an obligation of sorts to the children—but certainly not one that included dedicating nine years of his life to them. After all, it was likely that Sir Gerald was not the figure of horror that Mr. Dyer had made him seem. He was simply an unknown quantity.

"I think, Mr. Dyer, that I will be better able to answer your questions after I have spoken with Sir Gerald myself," he said. "And since I will most certainly be here through the month of January, we need do nothing sudden."

"Very well, my lord," replied the little solicitor gravely. "I do hope that you will make the decision that will be best for the Melvilles."

Lord Barrisford inclined his head slightly. "They will be a primary consideration, I assure you." He did not add that his own welfare would also be a primary consideration, but, as he looked at the gray-haired gentleman before him, he had the brief, uncomfortable notion that Mr. Dyer knew that he would do precisely what he had always done—consider his own best interests first.

"Honestly, Jeffries," he said hotly, as his valet struggled to help him into his dark dinner jacket, "to listen to that solicitor, you would have thought that I would consider nothing but my own well-being! I have seldom felt so put upon!"

"Shocking, my lord," murmured Jeffries soothingly, smoothing a single wrinkle from the back of the dark blue jacket that fit like a glove across his master's shoulders. "I'm sure that he says it because he has no notion that you are—all appearances to the contrary—a generous, giving man, never considering your own needs."

Barrisford wheeled to look into Jeffries' eyes. "You think me quite as selfish as Dyer does, don't you?" he demanded. "Although a man need not be a hero to his valet, I think that you should at least allow me my few virtues, Jeffries! I would not deliberately place these children at risk."

"No, sir," agreed his valet. "I can picture you sitting in the drawing room with all of them gathered at your knee, never wishing to be once more among the Greek islands." He sighed. "I can see you growing old in such a manner. I can see both of us growing old in such a manner."

"This is no time for levity, man! You realize that I do have to consider the welfare of these children, don't you?"

"Of course I do," replied Jeffries in an injured tone. "I have heard you mention that again and again—and yet again. Why do you think I would forget it?" inquired his valet, straightening Barrisford's white linen cravat with care. "Do you think me a slow-top?"

Barrisford snorted. "Hardly! If I were half so quick as you, Jeffries, I wouldn't presently be in my difficult situation."

Jeffries executed a brief bow. "Just so, my lord," he agreed sincerely.

"Well, I must go down now and face my fate," said his master restively, pulling at his cravat so that Jeffries was compelled to straighten it once more.

"Very good, my lord," responded the valet. "I trust that you enjoy your evening."

Barrisford cast him a suspicious glance. "You don't deceive me, you know. You hope no such thing, Jeffries. You are praying that I will have such a perfect horror of a time that I will rush up here tonight and command you to pack our bags so that we may leave immediately."

Again Jeffries bowed. "How well you know me, my lord," he conceded. "I had hoped that that very thing might occur."

"Well, it won't, Jeffries, so you may rest easy. I will have to work through this problem, little though I wish to do so."

And Lord Barrisford departed for the drawing room, leaving his valet sighing upstairs. Jeffries saw little hope of a reprieve for him and his master. They were fairly caught. And, thinking of Miss Melville, he feared that the trap might well become a permanent one. It seemed quite obvious to him, if not to his master, that Meredith Melville presented a far greater danger than any of the *femmes fatales* he had encountered before.

Lord Barrisford was talking with Mr. Dyer when Meredith entered the drawing room before dinner. She was wearing a gown of dark blue merino, a bandeau of the same deep shade holding her hair smoothly in place. To his annoyance, Barrisford, who had planned to be distant and formal, found himself bending over her hand and inquiring how she had been during his absence.

"Quite well, thank you, sir," she replied coolly, her

eyes registering a slight surprise at the warmth of his greeting. "It is fortunate, is it not, that we should have done so well while you were away? That will make it so much easier for you to leave us." Meredith had been more than certain that Barrisford would abandon them at the first possible opportunity, and she had been pleased—although a little unhappy—that she had been so accurate in her assessment of him.

"Come now, Miss Melville," said Mr. Dyer heartily, a little startled by her comment, "I understand that Lord Barrisford will be here through the end of January!"

"And after that—the world," observed Meredith, smiling without warmth. She had watched from an upstairs window that afternoon as David had rushed out to see Barrisford. She did not look forward to David's reaction when the end of January came. She was certain that the running away would begin again. "I'm sure that he will send us a line from time to time, always from the most interesting places. It is so easy to be responsible for others—from a distance."

"Would you like to travel, Miss Melville?" inquired Barrisford, determined to ignore the edge to her comments.

"Yes, Lord Barrisford, indeed I would. There are a good many things that I would *like* to do, but I daresay that I will not be able to do them. Unlike you, my lord, I have obligations that I may not turn my back upon."

"Well, I may assure you that you have at least a little traveling in your future, ma'am," he observed lightly, not allowing her to bait him. "Not to India or the Mediterranean, however—only to London."

"To London?" asked Meredith, for once losing a little of her composure. "And why would I go to London, sir?"

"My grandmother has asked me to invite you to visit her," he returned smoothly. "She will be away for a fortnight, but then she would be delighted to have you come to her for a while."

Meredith's face was aglow, but only briefly. Her happiness was snuffed out as quickly as it had come. "That is very kind of her," she said shortly, "but I'm afraid that I can't accept."

"But of course you can," he said in surprise. "You do wish to go, don't you?"

"Of course, I do!" she exclaimed. "It would be wonderful to see the shops and go to the theatre, but I am needed here at Merton Park."

"Nonsense!" returned Barrisford briskly. "I will be here and the Pagetts will be here. You will go to London and enjoy yourself tremendously."

Meredith stared at him for a moment, and then allowed herself to relax. After all, if Lord Barrisford and the Pagetts were here, why should she not have some time of her own? Why should she not go? Even Mr. Dyer was smiling at her encouragingly.

"Thank you, Lord Barrisford," she replied simply, unable to resist. "I would be happy to accept your grandmother's kind invitation."

Dinner was a happy affair. Meredith was smiling, a warm glow of anticipation seeming to light her from within. Barrisford was amazed that so simple a pleasure to look forward to should make such a difference in her demeanor.

She and Mrs. Pagett retired to the drawing room at the end of dinner, leaving Mr. Pagett, Barrisford, Mr. Dyer, and Evan to their port. A backward glance from Meredith made Barrisford determined to make the gentlemen's stay as brief as possible, and it was not long before they rejoined the ladies and listened to Mrs. Pagett play the pianoforte.

"Do you play, Miss Melville?" he asked in a low voice, seating himself beside her on the sofa.

She shook her head. "I have no gift for music," she returned softly. "Thea is the one who can play and sing—she does both quite delightfully."

"You are too humble, I'm sure, Miss Melville," he observed.

She shook her head decidedly. "It is a kindness for all concerned that I not attempt it. I hope that your grandmother will not be too disappointed in me, for I really have none of the talents that a gently bred young woman should possess."

"Even if that were true, Miss Melville, I am certain that you could never be found lacking. You appear to me to be all that a young lady should be."

Meredith stared at him in frank surprise. "How can you say so, sir?" she asked, startled. She stared pointedly at the scar on his forehead. "I'm sure that you of all people must know how sadly lacking I am in maidenly manners."

He shrugged. "Maidenly manners are greatly overrated," he observed. "You at least are never tiresome, Miss Melville."

"Thank you," she returned, smiling at last as she recognized his sincerity. "I can think of no finer compliment."

Barrisford looked at her suspiciously. "You know, do you not, Miss Melville, that it is indeed a compliment?"

She smiled, and a dimple that he had not seen before deepened beguilingly. "Thank you for pointing that out to me, Lord Barrisford. It is true that I have not received any from you, so it would have been quite easy for it to slip past me."

Barrisford laughed a little too loudly, winning for himself looks of reproach from Mr. Pagett and from his wife, who was still playing. He subsided immediately and attempted to be less conspicuous.

"If you would not mind, Miss Melville," he said in a low voice, "I told David that I would meet him in the library to help him select a book to read each night before he goes to sleep. I promised to meet him, and I expect that he is waiting for me already."

Meredith stared at him. "Did David actually *ask* you to do that for him?" she whispered in disbelief.

Barrisford nodded. "I had told him earlier that I enjoyed some of the old tales from Greek mythology, and he seemed quite interested at the time—at any rate, he listened to me and didn't run away. I thought that I would see if I could locate such a volume in your library."

He looked quite put out with himself for a moment—which was most unusual for him, since he never found fault with himself. "I had intended to find one at a bookshop in London, but my time was limited and I forgot about it."

"Never mind that. We do have books, sir," Meredith replied eagerly. "Please go to the library and see if he's waiting for you."

As Barrisford rose, she caught his elbow. "Would you mind if I come to the library in a few minutes to see how you are getting on together?" she asked.

He smiled down at her, surprised by the softness of her eyes and the her tender expression. That she loved her little brother he had no doubt.

"I would be honored, ma'am," he returned in a low voice. "I will look for you."

As he had expected, David was waiting for him in the library, curled up in a leather chair by the fire.

"Well, what do you say, sir?" inquired Barrisford briskly, looking about the room. "Let's see what we can find here."

Eagerly David leaped to his feet and followed in Barrisford's wake, trying his best to walk as his idol walked and to carry his shoulders in just the same graceful, careless manner.

Barrisford paused before a shelf and plucked off a leather volume. "Now this, Mr. Melville, is something that all young men should read," he said, smiling. "Don't be put off by the title—it's called *The Odyssey,* but it's full of monsters and murders and fights."

David took it eagerly from his hand, and Barrisford smiled down kindly at the eager boy, for a moment remembering what it was like to be alone.

"Do you know when I first read this?" he asked,

and David looked up at him questioningly, his dark eyes intent.

"No, of course you don't," said Barrisford, answering his own question. "When I was a boy about your age—or perhaps just a trifle younger—a letter came to tell us that my mother and father had been drowned at sea. They were coming home from the Caribbean and some estates that they had there."

David looked at him seriously, his dark eyes even darker than usual. The boy was not missing a word, but for once Barrisford seemed unaware that he had an audience.

"I couldn't believe it," he continued. "I had no brothers or sisters as you do, David, and when I discovered that my parents were gone, I was all alone except for my grandmother. I divided all my time for the next few years between riding and spending time in my father's library, reading everything I could get my hands upon."

He looked around him. "And this is *your* father's library, isn't it, David?"

David nodded, his eyes shining and his dark bangs spilling over his pale forehead.

"Well then—these are *your* books, David—waiting for you." He patted the book in David's hand. "Start with this one—you'll never be sorry," he said smiling.

As he walked to the door, he looked back to see the boy curled in a chair by the fire, reading steadily. What he did not see was Meredith, who had slipped in earlier and watched the little scene from a shadowed corner of the library.

"Well, Lord Barrisford, whoever would have

thought it of you?" she mused, smiling to herself. Perhaps there was more to the man than met the eye.

Nine

Lord Barrisford returned to the drawing room shortly afterward, only to discover that Mrs. Pagett was still playing, although she had now decided to favor them with a song as well. He seated himself quietly beside Meredith, who had reclaimed her place on the sofa without being noticed.

"So, ma'am," he whispered, "were you so charmed by the music that you could not tear yourself away to join us?"

She did not turn to look at him, but the glimmer of a smile lit her eyes.

"I am very devoted to music, Lord Barrisford," she returned. "You must forgive me."

"Perhaps I may be able to do so," he said, bending toward her ear as she kept her face resolutely toward the pianoforte, "but I am not so certain of your brother. I told David that you would join us and he was so intent upon watching for you that he could scarcely keep his mind upon what I was saying to him."

This did win him a direct glance, her blue eyes assessing him coolly. "Why would you tell such a tale,

Lord Barrisford?" she asked. "David said nothing of
the kind."

"Indeed?" he inquired in surprise. "And how could
you be so certain of that, Miss Melville?"

She flushed slightly at that, but suddenly would not
meet his eyes. "I was there," she admitted softly. "I
heard what you and David said."

"Did you indeed?" demanded Barrisford with interest. "And just what did you hear?"

"That you have a far softer side than you would like
to reveal, my lord," she said, smiling. "One would
never know—unless overhearing a conversation—
that you cared a farthing about anyone but yourself."

It was Barrisford's turn to flush uncomfortably.
"Well, I cannot say that his welfare occupies every
waking moment," he admitted, "but I must say that
I think he needs some attention from a man. He
misses his father badly."

Meredith nodded in agreement. "And you can sup-
ply that, sir," she pointed out. "You see how he has
taken to you."

Barrisford, however, was not about to allow himself
to be taken in. "It would be so with any man who
paid attention to him," he responded briefly.

"It has not been so with Mr. Dyer," she pointed
out. "Or with the rector who comes to see us regularly. Nor does he give a fig for Evan's attention."

"Give Pagett a little time," Barrisford began, but
Meredith did not allow him to finish. Instead she
looked him full in the eye, her gaze and her voice
scornful.

"What you mean to say, Lord Barrisford, is that you

don't wish for it to be you because you will not be here, and you have no desire to feel guilty. I quite understand. It is precisely what I would expect of you."

At that point Jenkins arrived with the coffee tray, and Barrisford was spared the need to respond. That was just as well, for a quick rush of anger had flooded through him at the cavalier manner in which she was disposing of his future by trying to make him feel guilty about the boy. David was not truly his responsibility, no matter what she might think. He would, of course, see that he and his sisters and brother were well cared for, but that certainly did not require his own presence. The audacity of her thinking that he would linger at Merton Park for the next several years left him momentarily speechless.

Barrisford accepted his cup from her with an air quite as frosty as her own, and the conversation over coffee was carried by Mr. Dyer and the Pagetts, with Evan inserting an occasional reference to the fine weather expected on the morrow and its suitability for excursions in the curricle.

When the party broke up at last, Meredith went across to the library before climbing the stairs to her chamber. As she had expected, David was still ensconced in the chair, deep in his book.

"David, my dear, it's time for bed," she said, touching his arm gently.

At first it appeared that he would resist her efforts, but when she added, "Perhaps if you get up early enough tomorrow, you could ride out with Lord Barrisford," he smiled and nodded, closing the book and rising from his chair.

Meredith sighed as she closed his bedroom door behind him and started toward her own chamber. What good would it do David to grow suddenly better now, interested in the world again—or at least in Lord Barrisford's world—if the wretched man were to take himself away in a few weeks? She clenched her hands together suddenly, remembering David's expression in the library when he looked up at Barrisford. She simply could not allow that to happen! She would have to see to it that he stayed at Merton Park.

When she came to her room, she paused suddenly as she placed her hand on the polished door handle. Perhaps there was something she could do. She had not thought of it before, but she might be able to make use of Lord Barrisford's interest in her. She did not flatter herself that he had anything in mind other than a flirtation for which she was the only available woman—Thea being, fortunately, too young, as Barrisford had been brought to realize. Perhaps, however, she could make staying at Merton Park—at least for a while—more appealing to him if she made him believe that she was also interested in him. Certainly she could not do it if she remained as prickly as she had been.

Straightening her shoulders, she forced herself to take the candle and turn toward Barrisford's chamber. Once there, she paused for a moment, trying not to consider the implications of what she was doing. However, if she had any hope of changing his mind, she would have to do something fairly desperate. She paused and took a deep breath, then knocked briefly.

That she had done something most unexpected was clear in Barrisford's expression when he opened the door and saw her standing there.

"Is there a problem, Miss Melville?" he inquired, certain that something of consequence must have happened to bring her to a gentleman's chamber so late at night. "How may I be of service to you?"

"Could you spare me a moment in the library, Lord Barrisford?" she asked stiffly, finding it difficult to meet his eyes. "I would like to speak with you."

"At this hour?" he asked in surprise.

Meredith simply nodded.

"One moment," he replied, turning to slip into his jacket. She noted that he was no longer wearing the dress clothes he had worn at dinner, but was now dressed in his riding kit, buckskin trousers and a blue coat.

"Are you going out, my lord?" she inquired in surprise.

He shrugged. "I had thought of doing so," he remarked briefly, offering no explanation.

They descended the stairway in silence, Barrisford wondering what the devil the problem was, and Meredith wondering what on earth she was going to say once she got him there. What had seemed such a fine notion a few minutes ago was beginning to take on all the signs of madness. How could she have thought that she would be able to convince a man such as Barrisford to stay at Merton Park when he wished to be gone? She was no flirt; she had none of the skills that a woman of the world could have used to bring him to heel.

As they entered the library, she left the door carefully open. Barrisford took note of this precaution and smiled grimly.

"I assure you, Miss Melville, that you need feel no fear on my account," he said. "There will be no repetition of my earlier lapse of judgment. You are quite safe with me."

Meredith smiled at him nervously, but it was a travesty of a smile.

Concerned by her expression, he put out his hand and rested it on her shoulder.

"What is amiss, Miss Melville? Has David run away again?"

She shook her head, cheeks flaming, not just with embarrassment but because she was all too aware of the warmth of his hand through the thin stuff of her gown.

"Where had you thought to go tonight?" she inquired suddenly—and more sharply than she had intended, for she was determined to take her mind off of his closeness and the sudden tenderness she had seen in his eyes. "Are you riding into the village?"

He nodded. "There's a full moon tonight and I had thought I might take advantage of it."

"Going to The Golden Goose, no doubt?" inquired Meredith drily, naming an inn near the village notorious through the surrounding countryside for its high stakes gambling and riotous drinking.

Barrisford nodded, more than a little annoyed that he was being questioned by this schoolgirl as though she were his great-aunt instead of his ward.

"I had thought that I would, Miss Melville. Do you see any problem with my doing so?"

"Not at all," she returned shortly. "You are wealthy, so it will not matter to you a whit how much you lose at cards. For Evan, of course, the case is otherwise."

"Is it indeed?" he inquired, eyebrows lifted. "And is Evan in the habit of frequenting The Golden Goose?"

"Often enough to be costly to us," she responded. "Evan does not have the head for gambling—but he doesn't seem to be able to see that."

"Perhaps I should look into the matter," said Barrisford thoughtfully. "Since there is a full moon, it may be that Evan has decided to take advantage of it as well."

"I'm certain that you will do just as you wish, Lord Barrisford," she replied briskly, moving so that he was forced to take his hand from her shoulder, "for you always do so. And if you can keep Evan from throwing away his money, I will be forever grateful to you."

"Now that would be something to aspire to," he said lightly. "I shall hold you to it, Miss Melville. I should like to have you very grateful to me."

He caught her by the elbow as she turned to leave the room. "And just why did you wish to speak to me, ma'am? We appear to have forgotten that matter."

Meredith looked at him blankly for a moment. He was quite right, of course. She had for the moment forgotten David and her purpose in bringing him to the library. Her impulse was to tell him that it had been nothing of consequence, that she had already forgotten it. Then she thought of David.

Turning to Barrisford, she smiled in what she hoped was a sincere and enticing manner. "I had hoped, sir, that you might take me out in your curricle tomorrow," she murmured, lowering her chin and looking up at him through her lashes. She had watched Anthea do it countless times.

It seemed, however, not to have the same effect for her.

"Is that what you brought me down to the library to ask me?" asked Barrisford, startled.

Meredith nodded stiffly, feeling every inch an idiot. How on earth did Thea manage to make this work?

"You need not do so, however, if it's inconvenient, sir. I'm sure that I will recover nicely from not going out riding beside you."

He stared at her for a moment, wondering what could have brought about this change of heart.

"I'm sure that you would recover," he agreed amiably, "but I assure you that I would not think of denying your request. I shall look forward to it."

"Thank you," Meredith said, smiling slightly as she looked up at him again. "I hope your evening at The Golden Goose is a profitable one."

"I have already had a very profitable evening, ma'am—after all, am I not to drive out tomorrow with you?"

Meredith grew pink. "You need not make sport of me, sir. I am aware that you could set any woman beside you that you wished."

He shook his head. "You overrate me, Miss Melville. I admit that there are a few that I could convince to sit beside me—but not so many as you would suppose. And I must confess that there is none that I would rather have there than you."

Meredith looked at him sharply. The words were flirtatious, but his tone was sincere. Could he possibly mean what he said? A moment's reflection, however, brought her to her senses. She considered it highly unlikely. What was much more likely was that he was making sport of her.

She forced herself to smile softly at him instead of snapping. "You are too kind, Lord Barrisford," she murmured. "I am honored."

Fiddlesticks! she thought to herself. She was positive that his honeyed words were insincere. He no more meant any of the things that he had said than she did. He was quite shameless! A moment more and she was able to remind herself that then she, in turn, must be truly shameless. She chuckled. What a ridiculous mess she was making for herself. She could only hope that she would be able to keep him here for David's sake.

As she turned again to leave the library, she was aware that he had once more caught her arm, forcing her to linger.

"Yes?" she inquired briefly, forgetting that she was supposed to be soft and yielding and glancing frostily from his hand on her arm to his eyes. "May I help you, sir?"

"Indeed so, ma'am," he murmured, his dark eyes glinting. "You were laughing to yourself just now. Tell me what you were thinking."

"Nothing that need concern you, Lord Barrisford," she assured him, trying to slip from his grasp.

"Ah, but there you are wrong, Miss Melville. I am very much concerned. "You laughed after I had said that there was no one I would rather have beside me in the curricle."

She nodded.

"Don't you believe what I said?" he asked.

"I think that you said the convenient and gentlemanly thing," she responded, "but not necessarily what you were really thinking."

"Do you think so poorly of yourself that you believe I would choose someone else instead of you to ride with me?"

"I don't think poorly of myself at all," Meredith snapped, annoyed by his arrogance. "But I can't think why you would say there was no one you would prefer when you know it is far from the truth."

"And why must it be far from the truth?" he pressed.

"Because you know that my pinching at you annoys you. You certainly don't find it charming," she responded frankly.

Barrisford laughed. "You're right of course, Miss Melville. You are like having a hedgehog with me at all times—there is no escape from your prickly remarks."

The truth of his observation amused her despite her determination not to be taken in by his charm.

"Scarcely a flattering comparison, Lord Barrisford," she remarked lightly.

"I was not referring to your appearance, ma'am, only to your manner."

"Then you will not be surprised when I ask you to remove your hand from my arm, sir," she responded.

"Not at all," he said pleasantly, "but first I believe that you owe me a kiss."

"Owe you a kiss!" she exclaimed, outraged. "What are you talking about, sir?"

"Simply this, Miss Melville. You drag me down here in the late hours and confide in me that your brother has a gambling problem and that you are unable to take care of it, thus throwing yourself on my mercy, for you know that I may go to the same den of iniquity that he frequents, and you want me to straighten him out."

"Just so," she nodded. "As his guardian, it is indeed your responsibility to help Evan before he gambles away all of his inheritance."

"How very tiresome it is, Miss Melville," he commented slowly, looking into her eyes, "to be in charge of doing so many unpleasant things. If you are asking me to do that, I believe that you cannot know me. I am not a man who commits himself to the unpleasant."

Meredith laughed. "I am certain that is God's own truth, my lord," she responded, "and it does me good to hear you admit it honestly. It makes you seem less of a snake."

He stared at her for a moment, meditating. "How to answer you, ma'am?" he said in a thoughtful tone. "How very humbling it is to realize that you think of me as a snake—though what do you really know of me, after all?"

"Not many things to your credit, sir," she responded.

"Frankness is not always an asset," he informed her gently. "It is greatly overrated."

Pulling her closer, he kissed her lightly, not at all as he had before. "I would not wish you to be disappointed in your view of me," he said, laughing as he released her.

"I have no fear of that occurring," she assured him. Then, thinking of David and her original mission of enticing Barrisford to stay, she smiled and forced herself to pat his cheek to soften the edge of her remark. "Am I still invited to ride with you tomorrow?" she asked in amusement.

He smiled. "As I told you earlier, Miss Melville, I look forward to it." And he bent over her hand and kissed it before leaving her.

"Enjoy The Golden Goose, Lord Barrisford," she called after him. "I trust you'll win. I can't afford to pay for your losses as well as Evan's."

Ten

Her warning was a timely one, Lord Barrisford later thought to himself ruefully. He had been unimpressed by the inn, small, squat, and plainly furnished, and had expected to see no one other than a few farmers, but he soon discovered that its clientele varied from well-heeled young locals like Evan to a few very older, very elegant men. He knew at a glance that at least one of those playing cards at the table nearest him as he entered was a Captain Sharp, there to fleece unwary gamesters. It was no wonder that Evan lost regularly. The miracle was that he had a feather to fly with after playing at such a place.

And Evan was there, of course. He waved brightly across the room to his guardian, undisturbed by being discovered and eager to introduce Barrisford to those at his table. As Barrisford was presented to the group, he mentally catalogued them: two other fresh-faced youngsters like Evan, still wet behind the ears; a square, ruddy squire, hearty in manner; a rather gaunt, haughty physician; and a slender, dark gentleman with piercing eyes, dressed in the latest mode. The last one he marked as one to watch.

"I won just now," Evan told him in a low voice as they went to the rather meager supper table in an adjoining room. "I lost two hands earlier, but I was quite certain that things would turn around shortly."

"Do they usually?" Barrisford asked curiously.

"Very often," said the boy confidently. "Luck comes in streaks, you know."

Barrisford allowed himself a small smile. "No, I was not aware that luck was predictable."

Evan nodded vigorously. "Oh, but indeed it's true, sir. I had thought as much, and Mr. Piercey quite agrees with me."

"Mr Piercey?" Barrisford inquired with interest. "The dark gentleman at your table?"

Evan nodded again. "I have played with him upon several occasions. He says that he has never seen a young man with such a natural aptitude for the cards."

I should imagine, Barrisford thought to himself. No doubt Mr. Piercey was always eager to welcome Evan at his table. There was probably no need for him to fuzz the cards with such a novice, and he would still go home with his pockets well-lined. Doubtless he was able to play fairly and still stay far ahead of the boy.

"Will you sit in on our game, sir?" he asked eagerly as they rejoined the others.

The others appeared quite willing for Barrisford to join them, although he noted with pleasure that Mr. Piercey looked somewhat less than gratified.

"I would enjoy it very much—as long as the others don't mind having a rather inexperienced player. I am afraid that I am no gamester."

The others assured him warmly that he was welcome nonetheless, doubtless envisioning some easy pickings for the evening.

And so he had seated himself and played for the next two hours, carefully losing just enough to make himself appear to be no threat. Mr. Piercey relaxed and, as the boy had predicted, Evan won the next two hands. After that, however, his luck appeared to disappear and he lost a substantial amount. Barrisford lost more modestly, revealing himself to be an inexperienced but determined player. By the time the evening was over with, their combined losses were sizable.

"I believe there is no need to mention this to your sister," Barrisford told Evan as they were riding home in the early hours of the morning. "I think that I am safe in saying that she would not approve."

Evan laughed. "How very right you are there, sir! But I must tell her if I am to get the money to reclaim my vowel. It is a debt of honor, you know."

"I'm not so certain that it is a debt of honor," returned Barrisford drily, "but I do realize that you must pay it. I will send Jeffries over with the money to cover your losses as well as my own. There is no need to inform Miss Melville."

"What a great gun you are, sir!" exclaimed Evan, his eyes shining. "I was afraid that you might not be best pleased to see me at The Golden Goose tonight—that you might even read me a lecture, as Merry does."

Barrisford shook his head emphatically. "Rest assured that I could never lecture as your sister does. It is not in my make-up. And I do know what it is like to wish to gamble a bit—just for the excitement of it."

"Just so, sir! I am glad that you understand—Merry doesn't, you know. She thinks that I should be satisfied just to go about my studies tamely, waiting for excitement until I am older. She has no notion what it is like to wish to be shut of the boredom of this country place!"

Barrisford, who was less certain that Meredith did not know what it was like to wish herself someplace more exciting, said pacifically, "Well, at any rate, we need not mention it to her. It will be taken care of."

"And I will repay you, sir," Evan assured him. "When I come into my majority, I will be able to clear my outstanding bills."

Barrisford was startled. "And do you have many—many outstanding bills, that is?"

Evan nodded. "It is rather discouraging, but I do have quite a stack of them. It seems so mean to keep me on a cheese-paring quarterly allowance that barely covers my expenses when I will come into so much more on my twenty-first birthday."

"But, Evan, had you thought that your twenty-first birthday is over four years away?" Barrisford inquired.

"Certainly I have thought of that," responded Evan indignantly. "I am not a clodpole!"

"And I never thought you were," Barrisford hastened to assure him. "It is just that it seems a little dangerous to already have a stack of bills that must wait five years to be paid."

"Well, it can't be helped," returned Evan briefly. "I do pay my gambling debts straightaway, but my other expenses I carry on a tab. After all, it's not as though they won't wait and enjoy my custom after my birthday. Why should that prevent their sharing in an earlier portion of my wealth?''

A little taken aback by Evan's line of logic, Barrisford could only look at him, bemused. Perhaps Miss Melville had had more to contend with than he had realized. He wondered briefly if Evan had any more small secrets that he was keeping.

When Barrisford finally reached his chamber, eager to go to bed, he found Jeffries waiting for him.

"What the devil are you doing up?" he demanded of the valet. "I told you to go to bed."

"So you did, sir. And I thought of doing so. However, before I left your chamber, Miss Melville returned and left a missive for you." Here he took a folded note from the top of a nearby chest. "I was afraid that you might not notice it before retiring, and I gave the lady my word that you would receive it before retiring for the night."

"The devil!" exclaimed Barrisford ungratefully, snatching the note from his hands and unfolding it. As he read it, he groaned.

"Well, you might as well go on to bed and leave me dressed, Jeffries. There's no point in my going to bed at all tonight."

"And why might that be, sir?" inquired the valet inquisitively. "It isn't like you to do without your sleep completely."

"I grant you that I would like nothing better than to put my head on that pillow and sleep until midday. However, Miss Melville informs me that David is planning to join me for my daily ride before breakfast. If I go to bed, I'll have no more than an hour or two of sleep before dawn."

"I take it that you intend to go," remarked Jeffries impassively, scrutinizing his master with interest. This was a new set-out indeed. Barrisford allowed no one to dictate his schedule. If he wanted to sleep, he slept; if he wanted to ride, he rode.

"Of course I'll go! What other choice do I have? If I don't, the boy will be unhappy and so will his sister. I don't wish to stir up a tempest in a teapot."

"How very like you, sir," remarked Jeffries drily, "always thinking of others."

Barrisford glared at him. "I'm not the totally insensitive beast you think me, Jeffries!" he snapped. "I do from time to time concern myself with the well-being of others!"

There was a brief pause while the valet looked thoughtful. Finally, Barrisford could stand it no more.

"Well?" he demanded. "What are you doing, man?"

"I was attempting to recall those other times that you were speaking of, Lord Barrisford—the times when you occupied yourself with the needs of others."

Barrisford threw back his head and laughed. "You are getting completely out of hand, Jeffries. I believe that I shall have to find myself a new man—a more pliable, impressionable one."

Jeffries bowed. "Just so, my lord. I will go now to pack my things." And he started toward the door.

"You know better than that, Jeffries, so don't even try walking out that door. You couldn't bear having someone that offered you no excitement, and I couldn't bear having a valet that would allow me to bully him. Just bring me a glass of port and a pillow and I will make myself comfortable for the rest of the evening."

"Very good, sir," returned Jeffries, bowing.

As he made his way downstairs, Jeffries could not keep from wondering. What had Miss Melville done that had so rearranged his master's attitude and habits? She was a handsome enough girl, but he had seen far lovelier. Her charm had to be what he had early suspected—that she would not allow Barrisford to run roughshod over her. Just as it had worked for him as a servant, it appeared to be serving the same purpose for a possible mate.

Jeffries sighed. He supposed that soon enough he would have a mistress and they would all set up housekeeping in some small rural greenness in England. Gone would be youth and freedom.

Barrisford was having much the same thoughts—at least in terms of youth and freedom. He had wondered during the course of his gambling this evening just what had compelled Miss Melville to invite him to the library for a conference. Had it been about Evan? Or about David? Or about something altogether different? She was indeed a prickly, demanding young woman, but he found himself looking forward to their drive tomorrow—if he were still awake to be able to enjoy it.

Eleven

Meredith shook her head with satisfaction when she saw David and Barrisford ride out together early that morning. She had been uncertain that he would bother to get up after spending an evening—and more than an evening—at The Golden Goose. After a moment's reflection, it seemed to her that if Barrisford could be up, Evan could be, too. She had checked his room after Barrisford had left the night before, so she was quite certain of how he had spent his time.

"Good morning, my dear," she called cheerfully, jerking open the heavy bed curtains. It was an unusually sunny day and she had already opened the curtains at his windows, so a burst of brightness greeted his narrowed eyes.

"Merry! Close the blasted curtains!" he yelled, pulling the covers over his head and rolling back farther into the shadows.

"Ah, but it's time to get up, Evan," she announced briskly, wresting the covers off of him and ignoring his muttered imprecations. "Did you have a lovely evening at The Golden Goose?"

The stream of muttering ceased and Evan opened

one bleary eye to stare at her balefully. "You're not about to start in on me about that, are you, Merry? Because if you are—"

"Certainly not," she responded, staring at him in surprise, quite as though she had not properly called him to an accounting after his last outing. "Why would I do such a thing, Evan?"

Thinking uncomfortably of the money he had lost, he said, "Well, because—"

"Yes?" she asked, waiting expectantly.

"Nothing," he responded sulkily, falling back over into the covers. "But do me leave me in peace, Merry."

"Why, Lord Barrisford and David have already ridden out together, Evan. Don't be such a slug-a-bed."

At this he sat up straight and stared at her earnestly. "Did they take the curricle and the blacks?" he demanded.

Meredith shook her head. "They were on horseback."

"Thank God!" exclaimed Evan, collapsing once more. "At least he isn't risking the blacks by letting that child take the reins."

"He lets you take the reins," Meredith pointed out.

He shot her an angry glance. "It's not at all the same thing, Merry, as you very well know! I'm older and a more experienced driver than David!"

"But Lord Barrisford says that David has a natural gift with horses," observed his sister, "so perhaps that makes up for the years between you."

"I am quite certain that I also have a gift for handling horses," said Evan with dignity. "I'm sure that I've been told that I have good hands."

"Doubtless you do," said his sister encouragingly. "I expect that if you hurried, you could find Lord Barrisford and talk to him about it during the ride."

"Well—" he began doubtfully.

"I know that they're going to stop at the Walters' farm to see how Joe is getting on, so you could probably catch them there."

Evan began to rise very slowly. It was clear that his heart was not in it, however, and she decided to give him a little added incentive to move along and join them.

"I am just getting ready to gather some of my herbs to dry for the winter. If you don't wish to ride, perhaps you could come and help me."

"Good God, no!" he exclaimed, revolted. "I can't see how you can spend so much of your time with those weeds!"

"Those weeds, as you call them, can do a lot of good," she observed tartly. "You didn't seem to think quite so poorly of them when my feverfew tea eased your sick headache last summer."

"Ah, well, it's quite different when one is sick, of course," he said sulkily, "but to spend as much time as you do isn't natural."

"Evan," she said patiently, "if I didn't spend the time with them, then I wouldn't have what we need when there are problems with headaches or fevers or other ills that they can help to ease."

"I suppose you're right," he conceded, clearly not

wishing to talk about it any longer. "And now, Merry, if you'll give me a little privacy, I'll get dressed."

Satisfied with her work, she departed for the garden. She had not liked the pattern Evan had been falling into: gambling and drinking in the evening and lying abed until the afternoon. He could tell her that London folk kept such hours as much as he pleased. While he lived at Merton Park, she intended to see that he kept country hours, and—with Lord Barrisford's help—that he contented himself with country pleasures.

As she gathered herbs and placed them in her basket, she hummed softly and busied herself with trying to picture what her life in London would be like. Keeping the sort of hours Evan had indicated would be difficult to adjust to, but going to balls and attending lectures and visiting the shops held a certain allure.

And she would be able to go with her mind at ease. All seemed well in hand here. Lord Barrisford had made friends with David and both Thea and Evan seemed disposed to do as he wished, and then there were the Pagetts, of course—cheerful and rather nondescript but apparently solid and reliable. Indeed, the only chore she had remaining for her here, aside from getting her herbs and potions in order, was to do what she could to make Lord Barrisford interested in her so that he wouldn't take himself away at the end of January.

Accordingly, when she dressed to go riding with him that afternoon, Meredith chose a particularly flattering gown of China-blue and a chip hat with ribbons of the same color that tied beneath her chin.

"Why, you look splendid, Merry!" exclaimed Evan in unflattering surprise as he passed her on the stairway. "Where are you off to?"

"I'm going riding with Lord Barrisford," she said primly, preparing herself for his reaction.

"You're going out in the curricle with him?" Evan demanded angrily. "I daresay everyone except the cook is going out with him in the curricle before I do! I cannot think why he would rather be taking you than me!"

"If this is a sample of your manners, I think there could be question of why I would make the choice, young clodpole," said Barrisford, who had strolled to the foot of the stairs. "You told me last night that you weren't a clodpole, but your behavior just now puts you to the lie."

Evan turned scarlet. "I beg your pardon, sir," he stammered. "It's just that—"

"It is not my pardon that you should be begging, Evan," said Barrisford, unmoved. "It is your sister to whom you were discourteous."

"I beg your pardon, Merry," he muttered, looking at the toes of his boots.

"That's your notion of an apology?" demanded Barrisford before Meredith could respond. "You should *sound* as though you are truly sorry, sir, else there's no point in the apology."

"Yes, sir," responded Evan, swallowing hard. Turning to Meredith, he looked her in the eye and said, "I am truly sorry, Merry. I didn't mean at all that you don't look fetching."

"Thank you, Evan," she responded calmly. "I think

the point in question is precisely what I might fetch—but I do appreciate your apology."

Evan cast an agonized glance at Barrisford and said, "I hope that the two of you have a pleasant drive."

"I'm sure that we will," replied Barrisford pleasantly. "Miss Melville?" he said, offering Meredith his arm. "Shall we go?"

Meredith joined him cheerfully. She knew that she was looking her best, she was about to get away from the house and see the countryside, and she was ready to make the sacrifice of flirting with Barrisford. Smiling brightly, she allowed herself to be helped up into the curricle and took her place, ignoring Evan's woebegone expression.

"Perhaps, Evan, you could take Thea and David on a walk to Mrs. MacComb's house to see how she is feeling after her illness," she said pleasantly.

Evan stared at her, horrified. "*Walk?*" he asked. "Walk with two children to go and visit an old woman?"

Then he caught Barrisford's eye and added hurriedly, "That's an excellent suggestion, Merry. Of course we'll be happy to do it."

Merry smiled down at him. "Thank you, Evan. I've prepared a basket for you to take to her. It's setting on the table in my stillroom."

As they rode away, Barrisford chuckled. "I must say, Miss Meredith, I have seldom seen anyone as horrified as your brother. Your suggestion clearly did not set well with him."

Meredith laughed. "Evan believes that if you don't

ride or drive, you should not go anywhere. I can only hope that he's always a wealthy man."

The drive began in a peaceful and unusually pleasant manner. There were for the moment no open hostilities, nor any sign that there had ever been any. Barrisford, pleased with the way he had handled all of the Melvilles' problems thus far, contented himself with an occasional glance at his companion. One would never suspect that she was capable of being so short-tempered and demanding. She was a lovely girl and, when she was smiling or her features relaxed as they were now, enchanting to watch. Quite tempting, in fact.

He shifted uneasily, for it occurred to him that being alone with her might not be particularly wise. The kiss he had taken last evening—innocent though it had been—had been preying upon his mind. He knew that his grandmother would disapprove, never believing in its innocence for a moment. He wondered what his companion had thought of it, for she had not flung his guardianship into his face this time. He considered that for a moment. Perhaps she had thought that it would do no good, that he obviously would have no consideration for her feelings.

He cleared his throat uncomfortably. Damn the girl! Why could he not just leave Merton Park and the Melvilles and return to his old life where problems like this didn't arise? He was unaccustomed to having to apologize to innocent young misses. Still, it had to be done. He could scarcely be calling Evan to book for his failure to apologize to his sister for his shabby behavior unless he were prepared to do the same thing himself.

"I hope, Miss Melville," he began—then broke off. There was a brief silence while she looked at him questioningly.

"I would hope, ma'am," he began again, "that you don't think that I was taking advantage of you last night when I kissed you or that I did so because you have no one to protect you."

Meredith caught herself before she responded as she normally would have, which would have been to point out that he was in the habit of doing just as he wished. Remembering in time that she was attempting to use her womanly wiles in order to tempt him to stay, she smiled in what she hoped was a beguiling way and shook her head, then averted her face.

Having prepared himself for a sharp rejoinder, Barrisford was a little taken aback by her reaction. Fearing that she wasn't telling him the truth, he stopped the curricle beside a small spinney and gently turned her face toward him.

"This isn't like you, Miss Melville," he said doubtfully. "You usually tell me precisely what's on your mind. Is there something wrong?"

Meredith shook her head, refusing to meet his eyes. Finally, she forced herself to glance up at him coquettishly and say with a small flutter, "Although it seems very forward of me to say so, Lord Barrisford, I invited you to the library in the hope that you *would* kiss me again. So, you see, I am the one at fault."

Barrisford stared at her for a moment. This seemed completely unlike the Meredith Melville that he knew, but remarkably like all of the other young, kit-tenish women who had tried to ensnare him with their plots. How blind of him not to have guessed that she was just like all the rest of them!

Meredith, unaware of his turmoil, smiled at him again and brazenly put her arms about his neck to pull his face down to hers. Startled, it took Barrisford a moment or two to react, and her lips were already pressed against his when he pulled away.

"I think that we had best return to Merton Park," he said shortly, not looking at her as he moved the blacks into motion once more. "And once again, Miss Melville, I apologize for being forward with you last night. It will not happen again."

"No, it certainly will not," agreed Meredith, deeply mortified by his rejection of her. "Your grandmother is sending her coach for me on Monday, and I will be leaving for London. You will be quite safe from me."

"You should do well in London," he remarked coolly. "Young women who are husband-hunting are often hurt by being too shy—it is the brazen ones that do well for themselves."

Meredith was almost too angry to speak and, if she could have taken the whip from him, she would have used it on him gladly. As it was, she swallowed hard, then said coldly, "I am sure that you know all about brazen young women, my lord. I am equally sure, how-ever, that few of them have my motive for their ac-tions."

"Your motive!" he exclaimed. "And what could that be, I wonder, if not to marry a title and settle me permanently in England?"

Meredith felt as though she had been struck. Too much of what he had just accused her of was true for her to bear it. Angrily, she felt hot tears begin to slide down her cheeks. Only when words failed her did she ever give way to tears.

In a final attempt to reclaim her dignity, she said as calmly as she could, "If it is any comfort to you, Lord Barrisford, I do not want your title—nor, if the truth were told, do I really want you. What I need, however, is your physical presence at Merton Park so that we may remain there and so that David will be happy."

Barrisford felt as though he had just suffered a brief but icy shower. "And so, Miss Melville, you are saying that you have no personal interest in me whatsoever?"

Meredith nodded. "None whatsoever—although I realize that that must be a blow to you."

It was, in truth, a real blow to his ego. His physical presence was needed and he was vital to the happiness of a nine-year-old—but that was all. Miss Melville apparently had no real interest in him. He was simply the solution to her problem

"And I take it then, Miss Melville, that you were prepared to offer yourself as a sort of sacrifice on the altar of family love?" he demanded angrily.

Meredith nodded. "That is as accurate a way to put it as any," she agreed.

The rest of the drive home was a silent one, stiff with anger and embarrassment. Each of them had been deeply humiliated, and neither of them was inclined to forgive.

"Thank you for the ride, sir," she said coolly a
Jenkins helped her from the curricle upon their re
turn. "If you will excuse me, I have a good many
things to do to prepare for my journey."

Barrisford bowed. "Of course, ma'am. The ride was
my pleasure."

And so each went a different way, both the victims
of injured pride. Meredith went to begin her packing
for London and to rail against the arrogance of men,
Barrisford to speak with Evan about the necessity of
avoiding high stakes play at any gambling estab
lishment and of avoiding fickle women at all costs.

Twelve

When Barrisford suggested to Evan that they return to The Golden Goose that evening, the young man was understandably surprised.

"I thought that I was supposed to avoid playing for high stakes, sir," he returned, puzzled.

"And so you are, Evan," Barrisford assured him. "I want you to play for chicken stakes, but I want to study your playing—and I want to watch the table."

"Study my playing?" asked Evan, more lost than ever. "Are you going to help me improve my game? I thought you said last night that you aren't very experienced with gambling."

"That was a slight untruth, Evan. I am reasonably adept at cards, but I wanted to watch how others were playing. Tonight I want to concentrate on you."

Evan stared at him. "And when you said that you wanted to watch the table, do you mean that someone might be fuzzing the cards?"

Barrisford shrugged. "It's always possible." He did not want to demean the boy by saying that there was probably no need to do so. "I would prefer that you not go to gambling hells at all, but if you must, I want you to play for small stakes and I want you to keep your eyes open."

Evan nodded eagerly. "I can still pick up quite a bit of money—particularly if you help me with my play. And I don't want to be gulled."

"Of course you don't," Barrisford agreed. No greenhorn ever wished to be the dupe of gamblers— but a novice, particularly an eager novice with money, was their natural prey. It was to be expected.

Evan went down to the drawing room before dinner that evening in the best of moods. Knowing that he was going to The Golden Goose later, and going in the company of a man like Barrisford, and that he would be free of Merry's recriminations—all served to make him a happy man indeed.

Merry's frame of mind was less cheerful, and after Evan imparted the happy news of his plans for the evening, she singled Barrisford out immediately.

"How dare you take him back to that place, Lord Barrisford, when you know how much trouble he will get into? I thought that you were going to take some responsibility for his behavior instead of joining him in his gambling!"

"And so I am," he said agreeably. "I will be going with the boy and teaching him how to gamble in such a manner that he will not lose everything he owns at the table."

"That's all well and good, sir, but it would be better still not to take him there at all!"

"And that is patently untrue, Miss Melville. You have only to think about it a moment to know that you're wrong. Evan won't stop going to hells just because we tell him to stop. And if he won't stop, shouldn't he know the best way to approach gambling so that he won't be fleeced by every Captain Sharp in the country?"

Meredith thought about it for a moment, then nodded reluctantly. "I suppose that that is the sensible approach, sir," she agreed. "Still, I would prefer that he were doing no gambling at all."

"I quite agree," he returned, "but since he *is,* I think we would be wise to take precautions and teach him how to protect himself."

Mr. Dyer joined them at dinner again that evening, although his business at Merton Park and one other neighboring establishment was all but finished.

"And you will come to see me in London, won't you, Lord Barrisford, and let me know your plans when you have quite made up your mind?" he inquired in a low voice before Jenkins had announced dinner.

Barrisford nodded. "Naturally I will let you know as soon as I am certain." He paused for a moment, then asked reluctantly, "And if I do leave, precisely what will happen with the Melvilles? Miss Melville appears to think that they will have to leave Merton Park."

Mr. Dyer didn't answer for a moment. "Before I was aware of Sir Gerald's existence," he said slowly, "I had thought that if there were a problem with their guardianship, I would bring them to London and have the court appoint me to care for them until Mr. Melville is of age. That is what Miss Melville is referring to."

"That was a very kind gesture on your part," said

Barrisford with some surprise. Having just contemplated the joys of guardianship himself, he was well aware of the sacrifices Mr. Dyer had been prepared to make for the Melville family.

"We would have been happy to do it, Mrs. Dyer and I," he returned. "Our only son died of a fever when he was eight, so having a family would have been a pleasure for us."

"But now that Sir Gerald has entered the play, he would be the one appointed their guardian if I withdraw?"

Mr. Dyer nodded. "I'm afraid that's true. I haven't mentioned it at all to the family, although I suppose I will have to do so quite soon. They know nothing about him."

"Let's not do anything just yet," said Barrisford. "Miss Melville is the only one who seriously suspects that I may not take up residence here, and she is about to go to London to stay with my grandmother. I've already had my solicitor get in touch with Sir Gerald and invite him here for a few days."

"Here!" exclaimed Mr. Dyer, forgetting himself for a moment so that the others all stared at him. Smiling apologetically and again lowering his voice, he leaned toward Barrisford and said earnestly, "I do think you should reconsider this, my lord. Think of what I have told you about the man."

"I think that you are worrying far too much, Mr. Dyer," Barrisford assured him comfortably. "None of the Melvilles will know anything other than the fact he is a distant relative, and Sir Gerald himself certainly has no notion that I am thinking of not staying here.

He is only aware that he has been invited to visit because he is a relative. There will be no problem."

Mr. Dyer looked far from convinced, and it was apparent from his demeanor during dinner that the idea of Sir Gerald coming to Merton Park was troubling him deeply. Before he left after dinner that night, he drew Lord Barrisford to one side and again begged him to reconsider the invitation.

"Nonsense, sir. The invitation has already been extended and accepted. It would be boorish to back out of it now—and besides, we may find that all of the concern over Sir Gerald is misplaced. He may be a delightful, trustworthy fellow."

Seeing that his protests were going to waste, Mr. Dyer had one more private conversation before leaving. To Meredith he said, "Dear Miss Melville, should you need me for any reason at all, pray remember that I am always at your service."

Touched by his concern, Meredith smiled at him warmly. "That's very kind of you, Mr. Dyer, but I'm sure that we will do very well here. Lord Barrisford appears to have everything well in hand so that I need feel no qualms about going to London. I trust that I shall see you there."

"I will most certainly do myself the honor of calling upon you there, Miss Melville," he responded earnestly, bowing over her hand and then taking his leave.

Mrs. Pagett's program of entertainment was rather shorter that evening and conversation seemed to lag, so the Melvilles and their guests retired sooner than usual. Accordingly, Barrisford and Evan were soon on their way to The Golden Goose.

The faces there were familiar ones, for the most part, with Barrisford recognizing only a few new ones. Mr. Piercey appeared to be watching for his young pigeon, and he looked more than a little disappointed to see Barrisford there as well. Interest in the game began to pick up almost immediately, however, and several people gathered to watch.

Evan followed his guardian's advice and kept his betting low, creating a little chagrin among his fellow players, who were accustomed to see him waste the ready much more generously. When Mr. Piercey tried to urge him into increasing his bet after one play, Evan proved immovable.

Barrisford himself continued his pattern from the evening before, chatting amiably and losing steadily. By the close of the evening, he was a most popular fellow because he seemed to feel no ill will against any of those who were taking his money.

As the two of them rode home, again in the small hours of the morning, Evan said impatiently, "So tell me, sir, who was fuzzing the cards? Was anyone doing what they shouldn't be?"

Barrisford nodded. "When you play with Mr. Holt, the physician, I would be certain to ask him to use a fresh deck, since he seems fond of using his own cards to play."

"Are they truly marked?" Evan demanded.

Barrisford nodded. "Although you have to have a sharper eye than I do to be certain, it appeared to me that they were. We shall know for sure before this is all over, however."

"Do you mean that we will go again?" Evan demanded joyfully.

"To be sure," responded Barrisford. "Only please don't act so overjoyed about it when you are in your sister's presence. You know her feelings on the subject."

"Don't I though?" said Evan a little bitterly.

"Which is why you won't aggravate the situation by bringing up the subject. Agreed?"

Evan was clearly torn, but he finally conceded with reasonable grace.

The next day, however, Meredith appeared too engrossed in her own preparations for her trip to London to pay attention to him.

"I believe that I could stand right next to her and announce that I had just gambled away Merton Park and she would just say 'Really, dear? Do be careful.' and go on about her business."

Barrisford nodded. "She is looking forward to her trip. It hardly seems fair that your sister hasn't been able to have her Season yet. At least she will have an opportunity to spend a little time in London."

Evan sniffed. "It's more than time that Merry acquired a little town bronze. If she did, perhaps she would be less worried about my behavior. I've told her that if she doesn't stop giving us all of her attention, she'll wind up an old maid."

"That must have comforted her," remarked Barrisford.

Evan grinned. "She picked up a pillow and boxed

me with it, but it's true, you know. At a ball, she spends her time checking on me in the cardroom or wondering where Thea is or if David has run away. She doesn't ever have the time to enjoy herself."

"What a grim picture you paint, you young ingrate! Don't you ever feel guilty for causing your sister to lead such a dreary existence?"

"Nope. I've done what I can to get her to take care of her business and allow me to take care of mine, but she will have none of it. If she doesn't have her hand in my business, she simply isn't happy."

"Perhaps she's just trying to protect you," observed Barrisford.

"Well, of course, she is, but that's the thing, don't you know? She wants to protect us, but we want to live and find things out for ourselves—not have our knowledge handed to us predigested."

"What an attractive way to put it," said Barrisford, grimacing.

"I do my best, sir," grinned Evan.

"I know that you do," Barrisford agreed with him. And that in itself, he thought was quite frightening. Miss Melville certainly had her hands full. Her sister and brothers could lead anyone on a merry chase.

"I say, Merry," commented Evan the next morning at breakfast, "will you be home from London in time to bring in the holly and the ivy for Christmas?"

To her dismay, Meredith saw that David was studying her attentively. She had dreaded the coming of Christmas, both because it was their first without their father and because his death had come so close on the heels of last Christmas.

"No, Evan, I'm afraid I won't," she replied. "But you and David and Thea—and Lord Barrisford, of course—will be coming to London for Christmas, so we'll be doing things in a little different manner this year. Won't you enjoy seeing London?"

"I should say that I will," said Evan enthusiastically. "I think I've spent about enough time in the country."

"Will we go shopping?" demanded Thea. "And may I have some new frocks, Merry, so that I won't look such a fright?"

"Yes, of course we'll go shopping, Thea—and you couldn't look a fright if you were obliged to," replied Meredith, pleased by their reaction.

David, however, was still staring at her intently.

"Wouldn't you like to go, David?" she asked gently. "You want to stay with the rest of us, don't you?"

He nodded once emphatically but continued to stare at her.

"What is it then, David?" she asked, puzzled. "Is there something you want?"

He nodded again and then, rising from his chair, he walked over to the fireplace and pointed at the mantel, and then toward the ceiling of the room.

"It's the greens, isn't it, David?" said Evan suddenly. "You want to put up the greens, don't you?"

David smiled and nodded, sitting down to finish his breakfast, and Meredith relaxed. Of course she should have realized that was what he was thinking of. On Christmas Eve they had always decorated the

house with holly and ivy they had gathered themselves, and David was very fond of the tradition.

"I'm certain that Lady Barrisford would not mind
if we decorated her home," she replied, committing
her hostess without a thought. If the matter were this
important to David, it would be managed. She could
not imagine that Lady Barrisford would be troubled
by such a request.

Pleased that David looked contented once again,
Meredith gave herself up to the pleasures of preparing for her journey.

Thirteen

According to Lord Barrisford's plan, Meredith would have been on her way to London before Sir Gerald Crawley arrived at Merton Park. Sir Gerald, however, had other ideas, and appeared on the Sunday before she was to leave the next day. To Barrisford's dismay that gentleman arrived just as he had entered the drawing room to speak with Meredith.

"A relative?" she asked in disbelief. "I don't believe that we even have any relatives," she said to Jenkins when he entered the drawing room to announce Sir Gerald's arrival.

"Nonetheless, Miss Melville, he insists that he is one—and I must say, miss," he added, lowering his voice with the privilege that belongs to old family retainers, "that he has the look of your grandfather about him."

"Oh, yes," said Lord Barrisford hurriedly, inwardly cursing Sir Gerald for coming too early. "I believe that I know who the gentleman is." He turned to meet Meredith's questioning glance with a smile. "He is a distant relative of your father, I believe—very distant."

"And how would you know anything about him,

Lord Barrisford, when I do not?'' she asked sharply, noting his sudden lack of ease and sensing immediately that something was amiss.

"Simply because of something Mr. Dyer said during his visit," replied Barrisford, forcing himself to relax and look casual. "He had mentioned that a relative had written to him after the news of your father's death appeared in the papers. That relative, I believe, was named Sir Gerald Crawley."

"How very kind of you to tell me about him earlier," observed Meredith. "And what brings him to us now?" she asked. "Why did he not come as soon as he read of Father's death?"

"I don't recall just what Dyer said about that. I would imagine, however, that the gentleman didn't wish to intrude," responded Barrisford deftly, inwardly cursing her habit of staying with a subject until she was satisfied, much like a dog worrying a bone.

"And how correct your imagining would be," observed an unfamiliar voice, deep and rich, "and I am afraid that I am intruding now."

The gentleman to whom the voice belonged, a tall, well-made man with thick dark hair, was standing in the doorway with Jenkins fretting behind him. Finally the old man managed to squeeze past him, and announced loudly, "Sir Gerald Crawley."

"Thank you, Jenkins," said Meredith, her voice quiet and self-possessed. Turning toward their guest, she extended her hand. "How kind of you to come, Sir Gerald. I am Meredith Melville, the eldest of Robert Melville's children. I must apologize for the shabby greeting you have received. I'm sorry to say that I was unaware that we had any relatives."

"As was I, dear lady," he assured her. "Not until I read of your father's death and a little of his family history did I realize that he and I undoubtedly had the same great-grandfather."

"Indeed?" inquired Meredith with interest. "I know very little about our family connections. Perhaps you could tell me about them, sir?"

"I would be delighted," he returned, bowing.

"I shall look forward to it," she assured him.

Turning to Lord Barrisford, she introduced him as their guardian. As Barrisford bowed, he said, "I apologize to you both for this contretemps. I wished for your identity to be a surprise, Sir Gerald, but I had planned to prepare the family for a visitor. Your arrival took me by surprise since I hadn't thought you would be here before Wednesday."

"Since this seems to be the time for apologies, I am the one in the wrong, sir," replied Sir Gerald. "I had business in the neighborhood, however, and rather than return home, which is a full day's journey, I decided to break my trip here."

"Now that you're here, you must stay, Sir Gerald," insisted Meredith, smiling. "Jenkins, if you will show Sir Gerald to the Blue Room, please." Turning back to her guest, she held out her hand. "How very nice to have you here, sir. Please join us after you have had a chance to rest."

Sir Gerald bowed and left the room. As the door closed behind him, Meredith turned sharply to Lord Barrisford. "So you invited him here, Lord Barrisford? And you invited him for Wednesday, after you knew I would be gone? Why is that, sir?"

Lord Barrisford looked more and more uncomfortable. "I did invite him, of course," he admitted, "but I didn't know at the time that you would be leaving quite so soon."

"You knew the approximate time that I would be going to London," she said brusquely, "and you have made no effort to tell me about his visit. Why did you invite him? It wasn't simply a surprise for our pleasure, I'm sure."

"When I discovered that you have a relative, I naturally thought it would be a good thing for all of you to meet him."

"I don't believe it was simply that," she responded, "and I cannot see why you would choose to surprise us. Even if your inviting him for Wednesday was done before my departure date was set, you could have told me of his visit."

She stared at him suspiciously for a moment when he did not answer. "I am too out of sorts to be dealt with in this manner, my lord. If you happen to recall any other surprises that you will be delighting us with, I will be in my chamber packing."

She was pacing about her room, angrily selecting clothes for her visit, when someone rapped on the door a few minutes later.

"Go away! I'm tired!" she called, not desiring to talk to Barrisford or to sort out problems for her family.

"Miss Melville—please do let me in. I've come a goodly distance to talk to you—and I would like to see you privately before we meet the rest of the family."

Recognizing Sir Gerald's voice, she hurried to the door and opened it.

"Thank you, ma'am," he said bowing.

He was indeed a fine-looking man, thought Meredith almost unwillingly—and Jenkins was right about his having the look of their grandfather. The portrait of him as a young man hung in the library, and Sir Gerald had the same dark hair and eyes and the hawk-like nose.

Meredith had a small sitting room adjoining her bedchamber, and she led Sir Gerald there to be seated.

"Lord Barrisford clearly has not mentioned to you the purpose of my visit. When I saw you come up the stairs, I decided to seize the moment to tell you in private."

"I appreciate your frankness," replied Meredith. "It is refreshing to have someone tell me what is taking place."

"But of course you should know," said Sir Gerald earnestly. "When I wrote to your solicitor soon after your father's death, I offered my services in any capacity I might be needed, including that of guardian."

"How very kind of you," returned Meredith automatically, her mind racing. That, of course, would explain the reason for Barrisford's invitation—and his reason for not wishing her to know about it. He was still planning to relinquish his guardianship, and he was looking for a way to do it with an untroubled conscience.

"Mr. Dyer wrote back to me at the time, thanking me and assuring me that your father had made arrangements for you before his death. I was surprised, of course, but delighted to receive a letter from Lord Barrisford inviting me to visit and meet the family."

He scrutinized her face, which had turned pink at the mention of guardianship. "Is there something wrong, Miss Melville? Have I said something to upset you?"

"No, of course not, Sir Gerald," she said, standing to indicate that their visit was at an end. "You are very gracious to make this journey to meet us. We will look forward to hearing more about you."

Sir Gerald also stood and bowed. "It is my pleasure, Miss Melville," he assured her. "And I stand ready to do your bidding. You have only to instruct me."

How very refreshing, thought Meredith as she saw him to the door, to hear a man ask for her instructions instead of attempting to order her about or to arrange her life for her. Already she liked Sir Gerald—simply through comparison to the odious, highhanded Barrisford. Perhaps David will take a liking to him, too, she thought hopefully.

David, however, appeared relatively uninterested in their guest, as did Evan when he discovered that Sir Gerald was neither a sportsman or a gambler—and, to top it off, that he had arrived in a homely gig. There was nothing about him to interest Evan. Thea seemed to find him quite charming, though, and the rest of the family was relieved to have her assume the responsibility for much of the conversation with him during the long Sunday afternoon.

Sir Gerald did have countless family stories to tell— but they were all stories of his family and meant nothing to the Melvilles. Meredith herself was hard pressed not to yawn when he embarked on still another one late in the afternoon, and she was for once profoundly grateful for Thea's flirtatious manner, for she was studiously attentive to Sir Gerald's tales, while the rest of the family and Lord Barrisford were only partially present in mind, occasionally nodding vaguely and smiling when there was a pause in his monologue.

"I can't tell you how sorry I am that you are leaving tomorrow, Miss Melville," he said earnestly as she rose to retire to her chamber and dress for dinner. "I have been looking forward to talking with you."

"You must come again, Sir Gerald," she replied automatically, thinking how grateful she was to be spared a week of endless stories about unknown people. "I'm sure that my family and Lord Barrisford will do everything in their power to make your visit a pleasant one."

"They have already done so," he said. "You have all been more than kind, and I look forward to the rest of my visit."

Evan threw Barrisford an anguished look, thinking of what the next few days were going to be like—and also thinking that they would be unable to make their nightly visits to The Golden Goose during the time he was with them.

Meredith's mind was busy while she dressed for dinner. Although a trifle pompous and certainly boring, Sir Gerald appeared to be gentlemanly enough. Perhaps having him as their guardian would serve them better than having Lord Barrisford. Aside from her brothers' decided fondness for him, the earl had little enough to recommend him—he was self-centered and self-indulgent, given to women and gambling and horses—and she was certain that he would desert them at a moment's notice. The chances were excellent that the pompous Sir Gerald would be glad to make his home here—for she had noticed him inspecting the premises and the furniture and the silver—and he would very likely be a stable influence on all of them. Being boring occasionally had its merits, she reflected.

Another positive point about having him here was that she need not fling herself at Barrisford's head and risk rejection again, and the more she thought about this, the more important a point it became. There was absolutely no need for her to humble herself, she decided, when there was another and better option available to them.

She smiled as she smoothed the skirt of her green silk gown and carefully adjusted the curls spilling over her shoulders. Lord Barrisford had finally done them a service. Although he had intended to help himself, he had unwittingly helped them as well. What a pleasure it would be no longer to have to try to curry favor with the man!

Barrisford's eyes glowed appreciatively as she entered the drawing room. He and Pagett and Evan had been standing before the fire, deep in conversation. Pagett was a hunting man, and he had been discussing knowledgeably the joys of hunting in Leicestershire, his childhood home.

"The pheasant here are particularly fine, are they not, Merry?" Evan demanded when he saw her. "I daresay we could take out a hunting party later this week and do very well."

Meredith was profoundly grateful that she was leaving on the morrow. The thought of Evan with a gun in his hand had always unnerved her, and the problem would at least be in experienced hands while he was with Pagett and Barrisford.

"Yes, we have a goodly number on our land," she acknowledged pleasantly, "although my father seldom did much hunting here. Aside from taking Evan out occasionally to teach him to shoot, the game on our property has been left in peace."

"Except for the occasional poacher, I would imagine," remarked Sir Gerald, who had entered the room unnoticed. "That is always a problem where the game is plentiful."

"I don't know that we have any poaching," said Meredith. "At least we haven't been troubled by any problem of consequence. And if a few of the local people catch a grouse or partridge now and then, what is that to us? It isn't food taken from our mouths, and they may need it."

Sir Gerald frowned. "Nonetheless, that would be illegal, Miss Melville," he observed. "It should not be encouraged."

"I did not say that we encourage it, Sir Gerald— merely that it is not something that we trouble ourselves with."

Sir Gerald looked as though he wished to say something more, but Evan forestalled him.

"Please, sir," he said, turning to Barrisford, "do say that we may go hunting later this week!"

Barrisford looked at him with amusement. "And do you expect to have your kill for dinner, Evan?" he inquired.

When Evan nodded eagerly, Barrisford said, "Then we must be sure that the poor fowls aren't peppered with shot—that doesn't make them particularly appealing to the taste. In fact," he added, "the poachers who trap their game have better meals, because there is no shot to watch for."

"I'm sure that I wouldn't know whether or not poached game is better than that legally gained," said Sir Gerald stiffly. "I'm quite sure that I've never had any myself."

"Then you are unduly optimistic, Sir Gerald," replied Barrisford drily. "There is quite a brisk business done in poached game. I daresay that you have had it any number of times when you have dined at country inns or even in London—perhaps especially there."

Sir Gerald's expression indicated clearly that he intended to take issue with this view, but Meredith, not eager to listen to any more conversation on the subject, said hurriedly, "I expect that you will all have more than enough pheasant after you gentlemen have had your excursion, and our cook is excellent with wild game."

"It will be difficult to enjoy it without your company," said Sir Gerald gallantly.

Meredith smiled. "That's very kind of you, Sir Gerald. It is gratifying to know that at least one person will feel that way."

At that point Jenkins appeared, and smiling beatifically upon Barrisford and her brother, to whom this remark had been addressed, she took Sir Gerald's arm to lead them down to dinner.

Fourteen

It was with a sense of profound relief that Meredith took her place in Lady Barrisford's comfortable carriage early the next morning and prepared for her day-long journey to London. The Dowager had also sent her own abigail to accompany Meredith so that she would not feel ill at ease when they stopped at posting-houses along the way. In short, her comfort had been provided for in every possible way, and Meredith gave herself up to the unfamiliar luxury of being cosseted.

When the carriage pulled up in front of an elegant town house in Grosvenor Square, with torches burning on either side of the door, two stalwart footmen, both young and handsome, hurried forth to open the carriage door and help her step down to the pavement. Glancing at them, Meredith suddenly decided that Thea might not be so all about in her head as they had thought. Perhaps running away with a footman was not such madness after all. She chuckled to herself, wishing that her family could know what she was thinking. They would believe that she had lost her mind, for Meredith Melville was never frivolous.

The thought occurred to her suddenly that she might indeed be as frivolous at heart as Anthea was, but she had never had the opportunity to discover whether or not this was true. From her childhood she had been called upon to be mature beyond her years, and she had done her best to do what was expected of her. So busy had she been with that, in fact, that she had had no time to determine what she would truly like to do or, what was perhaps more important, just *how* she would like to do things. She had been serious for so long that only at the most infrequent of intervals, like the occasional ball, had she had the opportunity to behave in any other manner. At home she was always the responsible one, the one who had to see to it that the others did as they were supposed to do.

As she started toward the door, one sturdy footman on either side of her, Meredith felt suddenly free. The responsibility for the others rested on Lord Barrisford's broad shoulders for the moment, and there was nothing she could do for her family from London except to worry about them—which would do them no good whatsoever and herself even less. For the moment she would consider nothing except her own desires.

When she was shown into the Dowager's presence a few minutes later, the Meredith Melville who made her curtsey was not the same young woman who had left Merton Park that morning. She had undergone "a sea change" that had left her sparkling and light-hearted, feeling that a heavy weight had been lifted from her. Her family would have had trouble recognizing her, for even her walk had changed. She suddenly found it easier and more joyful to move, and her walk and even her curtsey were filled with life.

When Lady Barrisford looked into her eyes, she smiled—partially for the pleasure of looking at the young woman before her and partially at the thought that this one would give her grandson a run for his money.

"I'm delighted that you've come to me, my dear," said the Dowager, beckoning to Meredith to take a seat beside her.

"You're very kind to invite me, Lady Barrisford, when you know nothing of me."

"Nonsense! I didn't know your mother well, but I remember her. Vivian Reed was the beauty of her Season, and your father snapped her up as soon as possible. She was a glowing woman—it was said that she could light up a room—and you have her look."

"Thank you," said Meredith quietly, for she could have heard nothing that pleased her more.

The Dowager looked at her piercingly, glad to see that Meredith, although she colored at the compliment, did not behave in any girlishly coy manner.

The old woman smiled again. "I'm the one who should thank you, child. I have been looking forward to your visit and it has given me a new lease on life."

The next two days were a breathless whirl for Meredith. The Dowager rushed her off to a fashionable mantua-maker, and Merry was measured and draped with fabrics in such a rainbow of colors and textures and weights that she began to grow dizzy. Nor did the shopping end there. Indeed, she discovered that they were just beginning. By the time they returned to Grosvenor Square to meet the hairdresser, the carriage was brimful with slippers, sandals, pattens for the rain, gloves, fans, perfumes, lacy nightgowns and undergarments, hair ribbons and ornaments. When she had protested that she really needed nothing new, Lady Barrisford had eyed her sternly and asked if she intended to interfere with an old lady's pleasure. Meredith replied that she had no such intention, and gladly gave herself up to a life of ease that she had never known.

On the evening of her second day in London, Meredith attended her first rout. It was a relatively small affair, for the Dowager intended for her to be comfortable, but it seemed incredibly sophisticated to Meredith, who was accustomed to the simpler life in the country. After inspecting the gowns of the ladies there, she was grateful that Lady Barrisford had forced her to accept the gift of a new London wardrobe. She had no doubt that she was dressed as fashionably as any other woman in the room and, judging from the number of gentlemen who had requested an introduction, she need not fear being a wallflower.

An imposing gentleman named Edmund Adams swept her into a waltz, the daring innovation imported from Vienna. Meredith was grateful that her hostess had not overlooked the services of a dancing master who had come only that morning to instruct her in its intricacies. She devoted a brief moment to the hope that Thea would not discover the waltz for at least another year, but then the movement and the music—and Mr. Adams—forced it from her mind.

"You dance well, Miss Melville," he said, looking down at her and smiling, "but then I was certain that you would."

"Indeed?" she said, her eyebrows high. "And how could you tell that, sir?"

"By the grace of your walk, ma'am," he returned lightly.

"Very pretty, Mr. Adams," she said, nodding her head in approval. "Very pretty, indeed. And should I counter with something like 'I dance well, sir, only because of the firm direction of my partner?' " she inquired.

He appeared to be considering her suggestion for a moment, then said judiciously, "I think that would work well. It's possible, however, that the 'firm direction' might sound a little too high-handed."

"I can see what you mean," she replied thoughtfully. "One wouldn't wish to seem high-handed."

He shook his head firmly. "Most certainly not. To give the conversation a slightly different turn, however, I could say that I had been anxious to talk with you since first seeing you this evening."

"And I, in turn, could wonder just why you wished to do so."

Adams pulled her a little closer. "Not just because of your beauty, ma'am—for there are many beautiful women here tonight and beauty itself is no novelty—but because of your eyes."

"My eyes?" asked Meredith, a little startled. "What of my eyes?"

"They are so alive, Miss Melville—you have very vibrant, speaking eyes."

"And what are they saying, Mr. Adams?" she inquired in amusement.

"That, dear lady, is what I intend to discover," he returned, his dark eyes smiling into hers. "Even should it take years, I shall make it my business to know."

Laughingly she withdrew from his arms as the music ended. He was, of the gentlemen she had met thus far this evening, the most enjoyable. Some of the others were too aware of themselves—of their own importance or their own inadequacies—and some were too dull. Edmund Adams seemed a creature quite apart from them.

The next day she discovered, to her mingled delight and dismay, the London habit of calling upon those you had met the evening before. There was a steady flow of callers and flowers at Grosvenor Square. The Dowager was quite impressed with it all.

"You are indeed a success, my dear," she said with satisfaction as one of the maids brought in another hothouse bouquet. "I knew that you would be."

How pleasant it sounded, she thought. She was a success. Then she thought of her afternoon, spent with virtual strangers, mostly young men with a sprinkling of hopeful young girls and their mamas. She had made polite conversation with all of them, searching desperately for subjects in some cases. It had been, she thought, an afternoon wasted. However, when Edmund Adams was ushered into the room, her eyes brightened once more.

"How pleasant it is to see you once again, Miss Melville," he said, bending over her hand.

"And I am equally glad to see you, Mr. Adams," she assured him. "You come at a time when I am most in need of rescue."

"Of rescue?" he asked, frowning. "Rescue from what?"

"From my callers," she said in a low voice, for fear that more were on their way into the drawing room. "I am not accustomed to being obliged to talk to so many people that I don't know."

He laughed. "I can see that our London ways hold little appeal for you, ma'am."

"I don't know that that is so," she demurred, "but it's very true that I don't like to have to spend my time in ways that I find unrewarding."

"And what do you find unrewarding?" he inquired.

She paused a moment and gave it brief consideration. "Things that I don't like to do," she said simply.

He laughed again. "How refreshingly honest you are!" he exclaimed. "I daresay that you won't like paying calls any more than you like receiving them."

"I am quite certain of that," she agreed frankly. "I very seldom go calling at home, except in cases when someone is ill and needs me."

He looked at her for a moment, puzzled. "And why would they need you if they are ill?" he inquired.

"I learned a great deal about the use of herbs and some of the potions you can mix from them from my mother," she responded, "so many of the people who used to rely upon her now rely upon me."

"Indeed?" he asked curiously. "I never would have thought that you would give your time to such an undertaking—for I'm sure it does take time."

Meredith nodded. "Quite a lot—but I enjoy it. And I don't mind paying calls upon those who need my help."

"Do you have any problem talking with them?" he asked.

She shook her head. "Not at all. It's very enjoyable talking to them. And it doesn't matter whether they're rich or poor, old or young, man or woman."

"I was quite right," he said.

"About what, sir?" she asked.

"When I said that your eyes—that *you*—are so vibrant and alive. It is because you are interested in the world around you, and not simply in the gowns and the calls and the trappings of our world."

"Oh, but I enjoy those, too," she protested.

"It's all very well to enjoy them," he responded, "but to believe that there is nothing more than that is a problem. And a good many people here appear to have that problem."

"You don't seem to," she pointed out.

"Not at the moment," he admitted, "but that's not to say that I won't have it tomorrow. You can never be certain when you might fall prey to it. And so I've come to ask your help, Miss Melville."

"My help?" she asked, startled. "I'm afraid that there is no tea or potion I can fix for that, Mr. Adams."

"It isn't a tea or a potion that I need, ma'am. It is your company. I've come to invite you to go to the theatre with me tomorrow night."

"I would be delighted to go with you," she responded, pleased to have two things that she could look forward to—the theatre and his company.

As she went to bed that evening, it occurred to her that she had been gone from Merton Park for only a few days, and already it seemed as though she had been gone forever.

For Lord Barrisford, it seemed precisely the same. Meredith had been gone a mere four days, but they had been four of the longest, most nerve-wracking days of his life. Two days of being in the constant company of Evan and Sir Gerald had been enough to set him thoroughly on edge. Sir Gerald maintained a virtually nonstop monologue, punctuated only by unnecessary and rude remarks by Evan. Barrisford had begun to feel that not only would he not last until Christmas, but that even two more days of this would be more than he might be able to bear. In his wildest dreams he could not imagine what Mr. Dyer had thought Sir Gerald guilty of, unless boring people into a stupor were a crime. If that were so, he could be brought up on charges and put away permanently. Thea remained the only person who paid any attention at all to him.

Just as Evan had wished, the gentlemen undertook an afternoon of hunting. Barrisford had been at some pains to go over the proper way to carry and use a gun with Evan before that time, so the afternoon went smoothly—until the very end. At that point, a gunshot had wounded Pagett in the shoulder. A quick survey taken after stanching the wound revealed that the shot had come from someone other than their party. Leaving the rest of the group huddled together, Barrisford had examined the area quickly, sure that the culprit, probably one of the poachers Sir Gerald had mentioned, had taken to his heels.

What he had found had been far from reassuring. Instead of finding, as he had expected, evidence of some neighbor wandering where he should not be and firing inadvertently, he found a gun that had been set with a trip wire that Pagett had apparently stepped on, causing the gun to fire in his direction.

The discovery had been distinctly unnerving, not only because of Pagett's wound, but because of the thought that there could be more of those planted in the woods of the estate, and there would be no way to know just where they might be. Consequently, the woods became off-limits for everyone: family members, guests, and servants. Until they had searched it properly, Barrisford felt no security in their running free. Not even the dogs were allowed to roam.

A sense of vague uneasiness pervaded the household, and he had been hard pressed to determine just what the problem was. His most notable loss was the company of Meredith, for no one else held any particular interest for him. Nor, for that matter, did anyone have any suggestions to make about the present problem that were helpful or even reasonable.

How had she withstood years of this, Barrisford wondered. Perhaps things had been better before her father's death, but, if his experience were anything to judge by, since then they had unquestionably been enough to bring on madness. He and three of the men he had handpicked from the footmen and the stablehands as the most careful and most clearwitted had taken to the woods to see if there were any additional pitfalls. They had found two more guns with trip wires and one man-trap, a cage the size of a man with a trap set to spring that would do substantial damage to the person caught.

They had taken all of these away, and he hoped devoutly that there were no more. The question preying upon his mind now was just who had planted these and why. Clearly Meredith had had no hand in it, and Evan knew nothing at all of what these devices were. Everything had to be explained to him. Who, then, would have been guilty of setting such potentially death-threatening snares? Barrisford was mystified and Sir Gerald was outraged—and loudly so.

This would have been quite enough to make Barrisford fear for his sanity, but another blow fell all too soon. While he was occupied with trying to solve the mystery of the poaching-in-reverse, that is, determining who could be setting the traps when the owners of the property were not doing so, Sir Gerald had been all too busy.

After spending an unfruitful day searching the woods, Barrisford collapsed in his bed, exhausted. To his displeasure, Evan appeared in the doorway of his bedchamber the next morning at an hour far too early to be considered socially acceptable.

"David is gone again, Lord Barrisford," Evan informed him. "Riggs came and woke me up just now. He hasn't been in his bed. He put pillows in his place again and ran away."

Barrisford sat up almost dizzily. The past few days had taken their toll on him.

"Gone?" he asked blankly. "Why would he have run away?"

"Just what we have wondered for some time, sir," agreed Evan readily. "I thought perhaps it was all over with when you came, but it appears not."

Barrisford staggered to his feet, taking a mental inventory of David and his favored places for running away. Clearly the roof must be checked—and he would have Jeffries check his wardrobe for any missing items. And fire, he reminded himself groggily. If David were angry, he could be setting a fire anywhere. He glanced hastily about his chamber, but sighted no puffs of smoke.

"Jeffries, what do you think?" he demanded, as his valet appeared half-dressed and yawning in response to his bell. "Where could David have gone this time?"

"David?" asked Jeffries. "The boy is gone again?"

Barrisford nodded, pulling on his boots.

"Well, you do have your boots, sir, so he probably hasn't gone to the pond again—unless he has taken something else." A hasty check of Barrisford's wardrobe set his valet's mind at rest. "Well, at least he hasn't destroyed something of yours again—at least not any of your clothing."

He studied his master's face for a moment. "But what do you suppose set him off?" Jeffries inquired. "He has been perfectly peaceful as long as he has had you to ride with and talk to."

Barrisford sat down suddenly and ran his hands through his hair impatiently. "That's it, of course!" he exclaimed. "How could I have been such a fool?"

Jeffries, who was waiting for enlightenment, ventured no opinion upon this interesting question.

"I'd been busy with searching the woods, which he wasn't allowed to do—nor was Sir Gerald. When I came back to the house yesterday, the two of them were together in the library. When they came out, David wouldn't look at me or speak to me. I thought he was angry because I wouldn't let him go to the woods with me."

Jeffries looked at him questioningly. "But now you believe it is because—?"

"Because Sir Gerald got a great deal too busy and told David that he might become his guardian if I leave!" Barrisford groaned. "The man has no sense and he talks all the time. It's Lombard Street to a China orange that the man has gone and told David that I'm leaving."

"Are we?" inquired Jeffries with interest. "I had no idea, sir."

"Nothing is decided as yet," fumed Barrisford. "I daresay it was just Sir Gerald with his tongue loose at both ends. I had told him that he was to say nothing—particularly to the children."

Sir Gerald was somewhat less than delighted by the intrusion into his bedchamber at what he termed an indecent hour.

"Really, Lord Barrisford!" he exclaimed crossly. "What can be important enough to drag me from my bed at this time of the night?"

"David," returned Barrisford, who was brief if not enlightening. "What did you tell him, sir?"

"What did I tell him about what?" demanded Sir Gerald, his face buried in his pillow.

"About becoming his guardian," returned Barrisford. "Tell me quickly before I lose my patience, man! The boy is gone!"

Sir Gerald sat up and stared at the intruder. "Gone?" he said blankly. "Why should he be gone?"

"Did you tell him I was leaving and that you were to become his guardian?" demanded Barrisford.

"Well, I might have said something to that effect," hedged Sir Gerald.

"You did!" exclaimed Barrisford, catching him by the throat and throttling him. "You fool! Whoever told you to go about telling the children anything? Didn't I tell you *not* to say anything to them?"

Sir Gerald, whose eyes were bulging, had some difficulty in responding to this question.

Jeffries took his master's arm firmly. "You really must let him go, sir," he said crisply. "Just think how it will slow you down if you must stop to address murder charges before you can look for the boy."

"Very sensible of you, Jeffries," responded Barrisford, much struck by his point. He dropped Sir Gerald, who fell gasping against the pillow.

"You will assuredly *not* be their guardian, sir," he said. "And if you wish to keep your wits about you and wear your head in its proper place, I would suggest that you not be here when I return."

Sir Gerald evidently took him quite seriously, and began to gather his worldly goods hurriedly.

When Barrisford and Evan and Jeffries, accompanied by an assortment of servants, returned home hours later, there was still no sign of David. Sir Gerald, though, was gone.

"Where do you suppose he could have gone?" Evan demanded for the thousandth time that day.

Barrisford, who was leaning back in his chair in the library with his eyes closed, said nothing, trusting that Evan would decide that he was asleep and leave him in peace.

"I know that you can hear me, sir, so don't play as though you can't. Where else can we look for him? What are we going to tell Merry if we can't find him?"

This unpleasant aspect of their problem had occurred to him, too. If the boy were not found within the next few hours, he would have no choice but to notify Miss Melville and possibly to send for the Bow Street Runners. Things were getting completely out of hand.

Just when he thought that things could not possibly get worse than they were, Jenkins entered the library looking older and paler than ever.

"Lord Barrisford," he said hoarsely, "I beg pardon for troubling you, sir, but we have another problem."

Barrisford sat up quickly, anticipating the worst. And it was the worst that greeted him.

"Miss Anthea is gone, my lord," quavered the old man, "and one of the maid servants said that she left with Sir Gerald."

Barrisford sprang from his chair. "I'll horsewhip the man!" he exclaimed angrily. "Send for my horse, Jenkins!"

As Jenkins hurried from the library to carry out his order, Evan called, "I'm going, too, Jenkins!"

"No, you're not," said Barrisford firmly. "I'll not have to answer to your sister if I lose all three of you! You stay here where you can receive any messages that come—from any of us!"

Evan drooped visibly, but he recognized both the tone of command and the good sense of what Barrisford was saying.

"Very well," he said sulkily. "I suppose I might as well call for hot chocolate and biscuits and have them sent up to the nursery if I'm to be treated as a child."

"Try not to be pitiful!" Barrisford commanded him as he gathered himself together and sat down at the desk to scribble a hasty letter. "You will be the only one here aside from the Pagetts, and we need someone to represent the family—an authority figure."

"That is true," agreed Evan, feeling a little better and squaring his shoulders. "Perhaps I'd better take up residence here in the library so I can be reached easily. I'll have Jenkins bring me some coffee and brandy."

"Just coffee will do nicely," said Barrisford. "Send one of the footmen with this note to the address I've recorded. One of the Bow Street Runners should be here within the next day and I will be here to give him instructions."

Evan's eyes brightened at the mention of the Runners, and he settled importantly behind the desk when Barrisford vacated it.

As Barrisford rode away from Merton Park in the gathering darkness, he could see Evan and Jenkins standing together on the front steps, watching him. He hoped devoutly that when he returned, he would be bringing at least one of the missing Melvilles. He could not bear to think how he would face Meredith unless he could restore both of them unharmed.

Fifteen

It was late on the following afternoon that Mr. Jeremy Bailey paid an unexpected visit to the Dowager and Meredith. The ladies were seated in the drawing room and looked up expectantly as he entered.

"I am glad to find you both in," he said, gravely shaking hands with each of them. "I'm afraid that I bring unpleasant news."

Lady Barrisford stared at him, for once shaken from her composure. Knowing that Bailey was the master of understatement, she placed her hand to her heart and asked unsteadily, "Is it Devlin?" For all he was a thorn in her side, he was her only relative and she loved him dearly.

Meredith was looking at Bailey fearfully, too. She did not associate Lord Barrisford with accidents or sickness, so it was difficult for her to think that he might have been injured—or worse. She felt an unexpectedly sharp sense of loss at the mere thought that she might not ever see him again.

Mr. Bailey shook his head. "No, Lady Barrisford, I can put at least your mind at ease. It is not your grandson."

He turned to Meredith, who stared at him with wide eyes. "I'm afraid, Miss Melville, that I bring the bad news to you. I was in Bow Street when a message came from Merton Park, requesting the services of two of their Runners."

"What has happened?" she asked in a low voice. "Has Thea eloped again?"

Mr. Bailey inclined his head briefly. "That appears to be the case. And she has left with a distant relative of yours, a Sir Gerald Crawley."

"Sir Gerald?" said Meredith blankly. "How could that be? He is, as you say, a relative—a guest in our home."

"I'm sure I couldn't say, Miss Melville." He paused a moment and cleared his throat. "I'm afraid that isn't all the news I have, ma'am."

"What else could there be?" Meredith demanded. "Please tell me quickly, sir."

"To be sure," he agreed, "I did not intend to keep you in suspense. It's your younger brother David," he said. "He has run away."

"But he stopped running away when Lord Barrisford came!" she exclaimed in dismay. "Whatever can have happened to cause him to run away again?"

Her eyes darkened as she stared at Mr. Bailey without really seeing him. "It's because of the guardianship!" she exclaimed suddenly. "Somehow David has discovered that Lord Barrisford will be leaving!"

"And where is my grandson while all of this is going on, Mr. Bailey?" demanded the Dowager.

"He is out looking for them," responded Mr. Bailey. "He is the one that sent for the Runners. Since I was present in Bow Street when the news was received, I thought it only right that I come to inform you of it, Miss Melville. I hope that I've done the right thing."

"Most definitely you have," Meredith assured him. "If you hadn't told us, I daresay that I would never have known there was anything amiss until it was all over with. I'm very grateful for your help."

Mr. Bailey bowed as he rose to leave. "If there is anything that I may do to help you, ma'am—" he began.

"You have already done it," Meredith replied. "Thank you again."

Bailey nodded and took his leave, and the Dowager turned to her. "We will leave at dawn, my dear. Can you be ready then?"

"There's no need for you to go, ma'am. The trip will be hard and everything at Merton Park will be at sixes and sevens. I'm afraid that you would be most uncomfortable."

"Nonsense," returned her hostess. "I would prefer to go and know what's going on than to sit about here and be forced to guess what's happening. Besides, my grandson may have need of me."

"He has need of someone—or something," said Meredith grimly. "I think he believed that he would be able to keep order at home simply because he was there. Perhaps he sees now that keeping order there is not as simple a matter as it appears."

"Devlin has always had his own way too easily," observed the Dowager. "I expect he thought it would always continue to be so."

"I expect he thinks exactly that still. If you will excuse me, ma'am," said Meredith, rising, "I would like to go and pack my things before dinner." She stopped at the door and looked back. "And I thank you again for going with me. You're very kind."

"Not at all, my dear. I would not stay home for any amount of money." And that was most certainly true.

As Meredith marched out the door, Lady Barrisford watched her with deep satisfaction. Her grandson had better look to his laurels if he expected to come out of this situation respectably. She by no means wished any harm to David or Thea, but she was inordinately glad that they had presented Barrisford with such a headache. It was time that he knew how the rest of the world lived. Never before had he been in a situation he couldn't control—nor had he ever before been fond of a woman he couldn't walk away from.

And Barrisford was most certainly in a situation he could not control. A search of the roof and the stable and a complete scouring of the nearby countryside had yielded not the slightest sign of David, nor had inquiries along the routes most likely to be taken by Sir Gerald been any more fruitful. The ostler at The Golden Goose had seen Miss Thea pass in her little phaeton with a passenger, but the Merton Park people could find no sign of her after that.

"All I need," he told Jeffries when he came home long after dark on the day of their disappearance, "is for the efficient Miss Melville to arrive and begin ordering me about."

"Don't worry about it, sir. Soon the Runners will be here and *they* will begin ordering us about."

"Thank you, Jeffries, for that very comforting thought." Barrisford eased himself into the hot bath that his valet had ordered for him. Neither of them had won affection by keeping the servants heating water in the kitchen and carting it up the back stairs in pitchers and cans.

Barrisford sighed in deep content as he leaned back in the water. "Every bone in my body aches, Jeffries, and every inch of my skin is filthy."

"Considering how you have spent your day and all of your evening, my lord, the miracle would be if you *didn't* ache and you weren't filthy."

"I suppose so," replied Barrisford, "but it somehow seems as though there must be an easier way to go about this matter." He lathered his shoulder thoughtfully and there was a moment of silence as he sank into both bathwater and thought.

Suddenly he straightened up and sent the sodden washcloth sailing into the screen that surrounded the bath. "Jeffries! Get me my riding clothes!"

Jeffries, who had been turning back the covers of the bed, hurried back around the screen and stared at his master. "It's almost midnight, sir. Where on earth are you going?"

"I am going where I should have gone first," he announced abruptly, snatching the towel from his valet and scrubbing himself with it as he stepped from the bath. "Why didn't it occur to me?" he demanded.

"I'm sure that I couldn't tell you," responded Jeffries, regarding with dismay the wreckage that Barrisford was creating. Puddles of water were soaking slowly into the carpeting, the damp towel lay on top of a handsome jacket by Weston that Jeffries had laid out just in case his master had returned for dinner that evening, and the washcloth had left a large and unattractive blotch of dampness on the needlework screen before falling into one of his boots.

"Just where are you going, sir?" he inquired. He made no effort to help his master into his clothes, knowing from experience that in such a temper he would allow no one near him.

"First to the stables to be certain that David hasn't come back there for his pups," replied Barrisford briskly.

"What are they doing there?" asked Jeffries. "I thought the boy always kept them with him."

"So he did—until now. He returned them to their mother before he ran away."

Jeffries stared at him, disconcerted. "If he's done that, sir, then he must truly be planning to take himself very far away. He is always with those pups."

Barrisford nodded grimly. "That's exactly what I thought," he agreed. "So it must be that he's left because he knows Sir Gerald was right—that I am leaving."

Jeffries lit up brightly. "We're truly planning to leave England?" he demanded. "I didn't know that you'd decided, sir!"

"I haven't!" replied his master tersely. "Don't pack the luggage yet, Jeffries. Certainly not now."

"Yes, I was afraid of that," sighed the valet, seeing his sudden vision of freedom fading quickly.

"I'm going to the Walters' farm," said Barrisford. "I've been quite sure for some time that Joe and his father are doing some poaching. I'd wager that's how Joe broke his arm and got those ugly cuts that Miss Melville so thoughtfully supplied the salve for."

Jeffries stared at him. "Poachers? You suspected that and yet you said nothing?"

Barrisford shrugged defensively. "I wasn't certain of it and at any rate it meant nothing to me. If they've been doing a little poaching to make ends meet and Miss Melville is willing to overlook it, why shouldn't I?"

"Just so," murmured Jeffries in a low voice, studiously ceasing his staring. Barrisford had never taken a kindly attitude toward poaching, yet here he was, apparently because of Miss Melville, as much as saying that it meant nothing to him.

"But even if they are poachers, why would you go to them now?" demanded Jeffries, having thought it through.

"Because they know the territory very well and they may know other hiding places David might use," replied Barrisford.

"And?" prodded Jeffries, recognizing that there was more.

"And," added Barrisford reluctantly, "because I've been afraid of having someone hurt by one of the traps set for poachers—like those we ran into while hunting. I want to be sure that nothing like that has happened to David."

He paused a moment, then added. "I also want to

know if the Walters have any idea who is setting those. They're certainly not being prepared by any of the family here."

"And so you don't really suspect Miss Melville or her brother of having ordered it done?" inquired the valet. He had seen man-traps before, vicious steel jaws that could maim a man for life, and he had no sympathy for those who set them.

"Of course not!" responded Barrisford crossly. "You know very well that they'd do nothing of the kind. But if the owners of the property aren't doing it, who else would have a motive?"

The trip to the Walters' farm was not immediately fruitful, however. Jeffries had managed to persuade his master that riding out at dawn would serve his purposes just as well, so it was at first light that Barrisford rode into their farmyard. There was no sign of David there, nor could the Walters help with any information concerning his whereabouts. They were, however, able to assure him that they knew of no more traps like those the hunters had encountered earlier in the week, nor of any others.

Joe, a handsome young boy of sixteen, stood in front of the fire, his arm still in a sling. "I don't think you need worry about Master David being caught in a trap, sir," he observed warily. Discussing poaching, even indirectly through reference to the traps, obviously made him uncomfortable. "The boy is too sharp by half to be taken in by such a thing. I know he's seen them before."

Barrisford turned to him eagerly. "You know that to be true, Joe? Has he talked about that with you?"

Joe shook his head a little reluctantly, clearly not wishing to talk more about the matter. "He didn't talk to me—hasn't done so since his father died. They're a new thing, the traps, though, and he wanted to know how they worked and why they were there."

"If he wasn't talking, how could you be sure he wanted to know that?"

Joe looked grim. "He came and took me by the arm and led me to one of them—a wicked-looking thing with teeth big enough to break a man's leg. I told him what it was for and to steer clear of it—and to watch for others. I couldn't tell him why it had been set out, though—except that perhaps the bailiff had decided there were poachers in the area."

"And are there?" inquired Barrisford casually, studiously avoiding looking at Joe's injured arm.

"There are always poachers," replied old Mr. Walters before his son could answer. "The man-traps are a new thing here, though—and they're as likely to get an innocent man—or child—as easy as a guilty one. We were surprised that they were put out here. Mr. Melville never favored their use."

"Nor does Miss Melville, I am sure," returned Barrisford, "and Humphreys never said anything to me about man-traps, so I don't believe that he is responsible for them."

The two Walters men stared at him. "Who else would set them?" demanded Mr. Walters. "Who else but the owner would care about poachers?"

"The very question I've been wondering about," responded Barrisford grimly. "It would appear that someone has taken it upon himself to set the traps

on Melville property." Here he looked Joe in the eye
"And if you're wrong about there being no more
traps, are you quite certain the boy couldn't acciden
tally walk into one?"

Joe shook his head emphatically. "He is too canny
for that, sir. You may take my word for it—I've seer
the boy in the woods."

"Thank you, Joe," said Barrisford. "You've taker
a great load from my mind. Now if we can only find
him and his sister—"

"His sister?" said Joe sharply. "Do you mean Miss
Melville?"

Barrisford shook his head. "We've been trying to
find Miss Anthea," he said reluctantly, sorry that he
had brought up the subject. "She seems to have left
with one of her relatives, a Sir Gerald Crawley, and
we haven't been able to locate them yet."

To his amazement, Joe had flushed scarlet and his
father and mother were regarding him with concern

"Miss Thea is missing?" he demanded, his voice
rising. "When did she go missing?"

"Just this morning," returned Barrisford, startled
by his reaction.

"And you're here instead of out there looking for
her?" he asked accusingly. "Don't you have a duty to
her, sir?"

"Joe!" exclaimed his father. "Remember your
manners, boy! Lord Barrisford knows his duty to the
family. You've no need to remind him of it."

He turned to Barrisford and bowed briefly. "I'm
sorry, sir, but he's been fond of Miss Thea since they

vere children. It would be a terrible blow to him if
something were to happen to her."

"My feeling exactly," returned Barrisford seriously.
'I wish to heaven that someone would tell me precisely where she is so that I could go and rescue her."

"I expect you'll find her when she's ready for you
o," observed Walters astutely. "She has always done
everything as she wished to. Running away is no dif-
erent."

Barrisford almost ground his teeth at this comment.
'Surely you don't mean that, sir. She must have more
sense of what is due to her and her family than that."

Walters shook his head. "If I may say so, my lord,
I don't think that she has the least notion of such a
thing. When she decides she'll up and leave, she just
does it."

"Well, surely she could learn not to," remarked
Barrisford. "I know that she's willful, but willfulness
can be controlled."

Walters regarded him silently, then said slowly,
shaking out the bowl of his pipe, "If you say it, it
must be so, sir, but drawing a rein on Miss Thea's will
would be a masterful trick."

"Perhaps she simply has never had a steady hand
to control her," observed Barrisford. "And certainly
her sister, who is scarcely older than she is, couldn't
be expected to do so."

"If Miss Melville can't do it, I don't think anyone
can," said Joe brusquely. He had retired to a far corner of the room after his last interchange with Barrisford. "She's steadier than most men and she
doesn't give way to temper as easily."

"Indeed?" murmured Barrisford, absently finger-
ing the scar on his forehead.

"Not that she couldn't use some help," added Joe
reluctantly. "I know that she works too hard and
never does the things that young ladies are supposed
to do."

He paused a moment, then said accusingly, "We
thought that things would go easier for her when you
came—especially when we heard that Master David
wasn't running away any longer."

There was an uncomfortable silence. Barrisford
had no desire to continue the conversation, but he
couldn't escape the feeling that Joe could tell him
something if he wished to. It was clear from the way
the boy looked at him, however, that he placed no
trust in him.

Finally Barrisford decided that he would have to
humble himself if he were to have any chance of making Joe talk to him. "He hadn't been running away,
that's true. I'm afraid, though, that he heard something he didn't like. He was told that I am leaving
and that appeared to upset him."

"And *are* you leaving?" demanded Joe, ignoring
his father's attempts to silence him. "That would upset the boy since he seemed to take to you."

Barrisford, reminding himself again that he
needed any information Joe might have, forced himself to endure this unaccustomed criticism. "No," he
said firmly. "I had thought of doing so, but I have
changed my mind."

Joe studied him for a moment, and Barrisford tol-
erated the unaccustomed scrutiny with fortitude. It

it brought him any news, it was worth enduring the disrespect.

Finally Joe shook his head as though he had made up his mind. "There's one place I know of where he might be," he said. "There's a deserted cottage set back from the road behind a spinney—he's gone there sometimes in the past."

"Will you show me where it is?" asked Barrisford gratefully.

Joe nodded and reached for a jacket hanging from a hook next to the fireplace.

Sixteen

The scene that greeted them when they reached the deserted cottage, some five miles from the Walters' farm, was not at all what Barrisford had expected. As they drew close, they could see a curl of smoke rising beyond the trees.

"Good! Perhaps he's here and has made himself a fire to keep warm during the night!" announced Barrisford, feeling suddenly optimistic.

As they slowly rounded a curve, carefully avoiding the deep potholes in the lane, they came upon Thea's phaeton leaning drunkenly on its side, one of its axles broken.

Barrisford's face darkened immediately and he quickened his pace. The old cart horse that Joe was riding tried to keep up with him, but failed.

Barrisford burst through the front door of the ramshackle cottage without ceremony, uncertain of what to expect and prepared to come to blows with Sir Gerald if necessary. What he saw stopped him cold, however.

Thea was bending over the fire, toasting a piece of bread, and David was seated close beside her, chewing his own toast thoughtfully. The thudding of hooves and knickering in the connecting room revealed the whereabouts of Thea's horse, and his noise had effectively masked Barrisford's entry.

"Thea! What are you and David doing here?" he demanded. "And where is Sir Gerald?"

They both looked up sharply, and Thea dropped her bread into the fire with the suddenness of her turn. Sobbing, she ran to Barrisford and wept into his cravat.

At first Barrisford could get little of her story, and he knew that David would be of no help. It was only with considerable effort that he managed to calm her and have her recount her adventures clearly enough for him to be able to follow them.

"And so you left Merton Park to look for David—not to elope? Is that correct, Thea?" he asked finally, wishing to have the whole matter clear in his mind. "And you were planning to go alone?"

Thea nodded, sniffing angrily. "But that busybody Sir Gerald came out and took my horse's head and said that he must come along too so that he could help in the search."

"And tell me again just how you got your phaeton out of its locked shed," he commanded.

Thea dropped her head. "I don't want to get anyone in trouble. A friend of mine got the key for me from the desk where you keep it."

That blasted footman, thought Barrisford wrathfully, promising himself the joy of an exceedingly angry conversation when he returned to Merton Park.

"And so you came here and found David?" he asked.

Thea nodded. "I drove to two other places first, but then I remembered this spot."

"And what about Sir Gerald?" he asked. "Where is he now?"

Thea hung her head. "Locked in the pantry," she said.

"Locked in the pantry?" echoed Barrisford blankly. "What is he doing in there?"

"We put him in there," said Thea, looking at David. "He may be our relative, but he is not a gentleman, sir. Why, we were no more than out of sight of Merton Park when he put his arm around me and wouldn't let go of me when I told him to do so."

"What did you do?" demanded Barrisford.

"Well, he had made me angry, you understand," responded Thea slowly, "so I took my riding crop and struck him across the face with it."

"Did you?" asked Barrisford, startled. "And what did Sir Gerald do then?"

"He fell over on the seat of the phaeton and started screaming that I had attacked him for no reason at all—which was certainly very far from the truth," responded Thea angrily. "I told him to be quiet and not to bleed on the seat covers."

Barrisford, who was beginning to detect certain family resemblances between Thea and her more formidable sister, coughed hastily and put his hand to his mouth to conceal any sign of amusement.

At least, he thought, Thea directed her violence toward someone who truly deserved it—an older man who was forcing his attention upon an apparently helpless young girl. A moment's further thought effectively killed all trace of laughter, however. He might as well have been describing his own encounter with Meredith. There wasn't a penny to choose between himself and Sir Gerald—a thought which unsettled him completely.

"And what happened then?" he asked, now suitably grave.

"I went to an old mill that David used to go to. There's a stream there and he fishes—and then I went to a copse just beyond the west side of our land. There's a meadow beside it where the deer gather, and I thought he might be there, watching them."

"And what was Sir Gerald doing all this while?" Barrisford inquired curiously.

Thea looked disgusted. "He was pressing his handkerchief to his face and moaning," she said. "He kept accusing me of disfiguring him—as though his face were his fortune, as it is for a woman. When we got to the copse, I made him get out and walk with me to the meadow because I was afraid he would take the phaeton and leave me."

"How did you force him to go with you?" asked Barrisford, trying to conjure up the scene in his mind.

"I told him that I still had the crop in my hand and that I would use it again if need be," responded Thea blithely.

"And I'm sure you would have," observed Barrisford.

"Of course I would have," she said matter-of-factly.

"He must have known it, too, because he came along quietly enough. In fact, he was really quite reasonable until we came here and the phaeton fell into a pothole and broke an axle."

"What did he do then?"

Thea shook her head in disbelief. "He leaped up and tried to take the crop away from me. He said that I was going to kill us both and that he wasn't going to be stuck out here in the middle of nowhere—just as though I had planned it all."

"And so you hit him again?"

Thea shook her head once more. "He was standing in the open door of the phaeton, yelling at me and reaching for the whip, so I pushed him to get him out of the way—and he fell and hit his head."

"Is he still alive?" asked Barrisford, waiting to hear that murder had been done.

"Of course he is!" she exclaimed. "How silly! A little blow to the head wouldn't kill him. David was inside and heard the noise, so he came and helped me drag Sir Gerald into the pantry because it had a lock with a key still in it. I was afraid that we might not be able to handle him when he regained consciousness—and besides that, as soon as it was light, David and I were walking home, and we wanted to be certain that he couldn't follow us."

"You wrong yourself, Thea," he replied. "I have every confidence that you could have dealt with him successfully. Indeed, I believe that Sir Gerald should be very grateful to me for rescuing him."

Thea smiled up at him, her lovely eyes still damp

with tears. "Now you are funning me, Lord Barris-ford."

"Not at all, my dear," he assured her. "If Sir Gerald does not remember me in his will for this act of kindness, he is assuredly no gentleman and hasn't a shred of decent feeling."

Thea's face clouded once more. "He is certainly no gentleman," she again assured him. "He's fortunate that I did no more than strike him with my crop and push him from the phaeton. If I had a father or brother to defend me, they would call him out immediately—but of course Evan and David are too young."

"And duels are no longer allowed," Barrisford reminded her, "but I assure you, Thea, that you will not be troubled by his attentions any longer."

"I should say I won't," Thea sniffed in agreement. "I daresay every time he looks in the mirror for the next few weeks he will be reminded of his beastly behavior."

When Barrisford opened the pantry and saw Sir Gerald, he could only agree with Thea. This was not an episode that the man would soon forget—or forgive. His face was indeed quite badly cut, his clothing torn and muddy, and his mood vicious.

"You little harpy!" he exclaimed angrily, leaping to his feet when he saw Thea's figure in the doorway. "You'll pay for this!"

He started for the door, but his expression changed ludicrously when Barrisford appeared behind her.

"I suppose she has told you some pack of lies!" he said bitterly, stopping in his tracks. "Why, the vixen—"

Then, seeing Barrisford's face clearly, he changed

his tone hastily. "I'm afraid that there has been some confusion, Barrisford," he said, trying to achieve an indulgent tone. "The child seems to have gotten the wrong impression of my intentions."

"I believe that the young lady had a very clear impression of what you had on your mind, Crawley." Barrisford stared coldly at the other man.

"You needn't look down your nose at me, Barrisford!" exclaimed Sir Gerald bitterly. "I know your reputation and you've no room to criticize me!"

"I don't believe that anyone has ever accused me of pressing unwanted attentions on—I started to say 'helpless females' but that scarcely seems suitable— on young women who have no interest in me," he returned, trying not to think about his recent episode with Meredith.

"Well, when I'm their guardian, I expect the lot of them will sing a different tune," said Sir Gerald, lowering his handkerchief from his face for a moment to look at the bloodstains. "There will certainly be no outbursts like this one."

Barrisford stared at him. "Are you mad?" he demanded. "After your behavior, do you seriously think that you could still assume guardianship?"

"You're not going to be here," Sir Gerald pointed out, smiling grimly, "so who else is there?"

Anthea and David stared at Barrisford in horror, and Barrisford forced himself to smile at them reassuringly; then he turned back to Sir Gerald. "I'm not going anywhere," he replied firmly. "And if you will have a seat, Crawley, I'll send someone back for you after we get to Merton Park."

"I'll stay with him," said Joe grimly.

He had been standing so quietly in the open door of the cottage that he hadn't been noticed. Sir Gerald twitched uncomfortably and dropped his eyes as he met Joe's unflinching gaze.

"That will be fine, Joe," said Barrisford with satisfaction. "I'll send back someone with his bags and you can see to it that Sir Gerald gets to town and gets on the stagecoach."

"But my visit is not yet over—" began Sir Gerald.

"Your visit is entirely over," finished Barrisford. "If you were to remain, I would have you up before the nearest magistrate for your conduct."

Sir Gerald flinched at his tone. "Well, I suppose—" he said in a disgruntled voice.

"You have nothing to suppose, sir. And if I ever find you within speaking distance of any of the Melville children again, I *will* have you up on charges, come what will."

The ride to Merton Park was a quiet one. Thea rode behind Barrisford and David behind Joe. Both were exhausted by their uncomfortable night and were nodding before they had traveled more than a hundred feet down the lane.

When they arrived home, Jenkins and Evan bustled out together to meet them, Evan electing to horsewhip Sir Gerald on the spot.

"I knew that you would feel just as you ought," Barrisford commiserated with him. "However, I believe that Thea has done a fair enough job of doing just that. Sir Gerald won't be attending any balls for some time."

"Really?" exclaimed Evan, his eyes wide. "Good for you, Thea!" he added, turning toward her and clapping her on the shoulder. "I apologize for thinking for a moment that you had eloped with such a maw worm as Sir Gerald."

"I should hope so," sniffed Thea, who had been horrified to hear that the others had suspected another elopement. "At least Merry wasn't here to misjudge me with the rest of you. I hate to think what a sermon she would read me about going out without permission."

"Lord, yes!" agreed Evan fervently. "If she were here, we'd never hear the end of it."

It was the next morning before they reached the unhappy conclusion that they had congratulated themselves too soon for keeping the whole escapade as quiet as possible. At breakfast a wide-eyed Jenkins leaned close to Barrisford and whispered something to him. Barrisford closed his eyes for a moment, then nodded.

"Show him to the library, Jenkins," he commanded briskly, and rose from the table.

"What could be going on that is such a secret?" asked Evan, watching their guardian close the door behind him with a rather too decided snap.

He rose from the table and started toward the door.

"I wouldn't do it, Evan," cautioned his sister. "You know that he won't like you nosing about."

Evan grinned. "Just a healthy curiosity, Thea. Like a cat."

"Humph! You know what happened to that cat, too," she returned, unimpressed.

In a matter of minutes, Evan came speeding back into the room, his eyes wide. "You'll never guess, Thea—never in a thousand years. The fellow's a Runner!"

Thea stared at blankly.

"You know what I mean!" he said impatiently. "A Bow Street Runner from London! Barrisford sent for him to help find you and David!"

"How did you discover that?" asked Thea.

"My ear to a partially open door," returned Evan smugly. "I'm afraid the fellow's out of a job, though. Barrisford is sending him back to London. I bet this'll cost him a pretty penny."

Thea nodded. "Do you think the Runner had asked anyone about me before coming here?"

Evan nodded reluctantly. "He'd made one stop."

"Well, where?" prodded Thea, after waiting for a few moments.

"The Golden Goose," he replied.

"The Golden Goose!" she echoed. "He might as well have put up broadsheets with my name on them!"

Evan nodded again. "I don't believe the fellow is particularly discreet," he admitted.

They looked at each other in dismay, but that bit of news was nothing compared to that of Barrisford, who had received a brief note from Meredith, carried post by one of his grandmother's footmen. She would arrive the next morning—with Lady Barrisford. He sighed, thinking of what the scene would be like.

And then he remembered something that he had

not allowed himself to think of since his return with the prodigal children. He had not, in fact, mentioned it even to Jeffries. He had promised that he would stay so that Sir Gerald could not be their guardian.

He sat back in his chair and stared out the window, absently watching a few flakes of snow float by. Last week's golden days in the garden were a memory. A hard, cold rain had stripped most of the leaves from the trees, leaving dark skeletons against a gray sky.

It was November. He was in England. He had a family to care for. He suddenly felt as bleak as the November scene before him. The world was closing in on him and freedom belonged to the past.

Seventeen

Meredith was feeling little happier. She and Lady Barrisford had left even before dawn, and her hostess spared no pains to get them back to Merton Park as rapidly as possible. They changed their horses often, and the Dowager pressed her with offers of refreshment, but she had little heart for them. Her mood matched the bleakness of the day, and she could not rouse herself to talk.

Instead, she thought of David and Thea and cursed herself for leaving them. She should have known full well what would happen. Leaving Lord Barrisford in charge had been an error in judgment, and she had made it simply so that she could indulge herself in London. Guilt welled up within her and threatened to drown her completely.

"Come now, Miss Melville, don't take so much upon yourself," remonstrated the Dowager, studying her charge. "It isn't your fault this happened, and Devlin will take care of it. He's fairly efficient when he must be."

Meredith shook her head, afraid to speak for fear she would cry. She was not prone to tears, but the

past few hours had taken their toll on her. Common
sense told her that everything would be all right—after all, Thea had eloped before and David had certainly run away—but she could not make herself
accept the more cheerful possibility. The fact that she
had not been there to oversee them personally made
her fear that this negligence would be paid for with
some awful disaster.

By the time they arrived at Merton Park, Meredith
was a nervous wreck—but an angry nervous wreck.
She had had time to think of the various ways in
which Barrisford's own negligence might have
brought about the present problem, and she was prepared to show him no quarter.

When the carriage stopped at the entrance of her
home, Jenkins hurried out to welcome her, and
Meredith clutched his arm. "What is the news? Do
we know anything of either of them?" she asked fearfully.

"Oh, yes indeed, miss," he assured her. "Didn't
Lady Barrisford's footman reach you with the news?"

Her bewildered stare encouraged him to continue.
"They are both home and well. Lord Barrisford sent
him back with the message that you needn't interrupt
your visit because all was well here."

"Did he indeed?" she asked wrathfully. As she had
told Mr. Bailey, she was certain that if she had not
received the news from him, she would have heard
nothing of Thea's and David's escapades from Lord
Barrisford.

"You see, Miss Melville?" said Lady Barrisford. "I
was certain that everything would be all right and

hat Devlin would take care of things. He is more
ompetent than you might expect."

"You overwhelm me, ma'am," said Lord Barrisford
lrily. The library door had opened and he had been
istening to the interchange.

Normally Meredith would have ushered their guest
o her chamber and seen to her comfort, taking up
her grievance with Barrisford in private at a later
ime. Her nerves, however, and her guilt had had
ime to do their work. Forgetting her duties as a hostess, she wheeled on him and spilled out the pent-up
ury of a full day and night of anxious waiting.

"If you were competent, Lord Barrisford, none of
his would have happened. Tell me, if you please, just
why David suddenly ran away when he hasn't done
o for weeks?"

"Well," Barrisford began, "it appears that—"

"It appears that he learned that you had no real
nterest in being here. Doubtless he ran away so that
he wouldn't be deserted again!" Meredith wouldn't
allow herself to think that the boy might feel that she
oo had deserted him.

"Come now, Merry, that's going it too strong!" in-
errupted Evan, who had been attracted from the bil-
iard room by the noise. "Why, Lord Barrisford has
promised that he will stay so that Sir Gerald won't be
our guardian. You could at least be a little grateful
o him."

"Grateful!" exclaimed Meredith bitterly. "And why
hould I be grateful? Whatever makes you think that
ou can believe him?" she demanded.

Barrisford stiffened. "I believe, ma'am, that my

word as a gentleman is usually acceptable in mos
circles. May I ask why you would choose to question
it?"

"The better question would be why I would choose
to accept it!" she retorted. "When have I seen you
play the role of gentleman? Oh, yes," she continued
eagerly, seeing by his scarlet complexion that she had
struck home at last, "I see that you take my meaning.
You have shown me, I believe, exactly what kind of a
'gentleman' you are!"

"Are you talking about that broken vase, Merry?"
inquired Evan with interest. "Precisely what did happen with that?"

Ignoring him, Meredith continued her tirade.
"And I must admit, Lord Barrisford, that the fault is
partially mine for having agreed to leave my sister
and brothers in your care! I knew better than any of
the others what manner of man you are!"

Not waiting to give him a chance to respond, she
turned and said in a cool tone, totally unlike the one
she had just used with him, "May I show you to your
room, Lady Barrisford? I am sorry that you've had to
wait."

"It's perfectly all right, my dear," returned the
Dowager with satisfaction. "I wouldn't have missed it
for the world." Glancing at her grandson as she
passed him, she smiled. "Not for the world," she repeated, patting Barrisford's scarlet cheek with her
gloved hand. "I am pleased to see you, Devlin—very
pleased."

Dinner was not a rattling success even though Lady
Barrisford, ably seconded by Evan, made a valiant

effort at cheerful conversation. Thea was somewhat subdued by Merry's reaction to her latest adventure, and David of course was silent. Barrisford confined himself to monosyllables and Meredith to cold nods.

"I hope that you will be staying with us some time, Lady Barrisford," remarked Evan politely, after conversation had died once more.

"That's very kind of you, Mr. Melville," she returned, glancing at Meredith, "but I would imagine since everything is in order here, that your sister and I will be returning to London as soon as possible. We have engagements there, and Miss Melville has already missed several of them."

Here she turned to her grandson, "You remember Edmund Adams, don't you, Devlin?" she inquired pleasantly.

"Yes, of course. How is he?" returned Barrisford absently.

The Dowager smiled. "Very well—and he is clearly smitten by Miss Melville. She was to have attended the theatre with him last night." She paused a moment. "I can't remember when I have seen Edmund so taken with anyone."

Barrisford was silent, but Evan's eyebrows shot up. "A conquest, Merry?" he inquired gleefully. "You're working very quickly. At this rate, you'll be married before we come to London for the holidays."

"Don't be tasteless, Evan!" snapped his sister. "Of course I shall not be!"

"And I wouldn't say that Miss Melville has limited herself to a single conquest," remarked Lady Barrisford, watching her grandson from the corner of her eye. "My drawing room is full to overflowing with the bouquets sent to her after Lady D'Anville's rout."

"You are exaggerating, ma'am," remonstrated Meredith, unhappy at having attention focused upon her.

"Not at all. If one more bouquet had come, Barton would have had no place to put is, save the floor."

"Well, I must say that I am impressed," said Evan, staring at his sister.

Thea, too, was looking at Meredith with wide eyes. "I had no idea that you had a taste for such things, Merry," she said.

"Such things as what?" demanded Meredith unwisely.

"Flirtations," responded Thea simply.

Meredith flushed scarlet. Precisely what Barrisford had said she would occupy herself with. She straightened her shoulders as she thought of him watching her critically. "I suppose you think that, Thea, because I never had time for one while living here."

"I suppose not," replied her sister thoughtfully. "I had never considered it before, but I suppose it is a drawback having us to care for. I mean, you didn't have a chance to go out as often as you might have otherwise because one of us always had a problem when you tried to leave."

"Yes," said Meredith drily, thinking of what had brought her back to Merton Park before having even an entire week in London.

Thea and Evan appeared to have had the same thought, and both tried to hurry into conversation immediately.

"Well, there wasn't actually as much of a problem—" began Thea.

"Tell us more, Merry," interrupted Evan loudly. "Tell us all about your adventures in London."

Taking pity on them, Meredith smiled and allowed him to direct the conversation away from troublesome problems.

Meredith and the Dowager stayed only one more day at Merton Park, during which time Meredith and Barrisford studiously avoided one another. On the second day Meredith rode down to see the Walters family and to take Joe more salve for his wounds.

"I want to thank you, Joe," said Meredith, extending her hand to him, "for helping to find my brother and sister—and for sending Sir Gerald on his way. Thea has told me all about what you did for them."

Joe flushed and shook her hand awkwardly. "I'm glad no harm came to them, miss."

"Thanks to you, none did," she replied, preparing to leave.

"Miss Melville," he said suddenly, walking after her, "may I tell you something?"

"Yes, of course, Joe." Meredith turned to look at him in surprise. Always quiet and rather bashful, he had never had much to say around her.

"Lord Barrisford asked my father and me whether we knew of any more traps set for poachers on your land—"

"Set on *our* land?" she asked sharply.

He nodded.

She looked at his arm. "Did that happen to you on our property, Joe?" she demanded.

He nodded once more, shifting uneasily under her angry gaze.

"I thought that had happened to you on a neighbor's property, Joe, and I never said anything for fear of embarrassing you or getting you in trouble."

She sank down onto the bench beside the door of the cottage and stared at him. "Who would set those on our property?"

Joe shook his head. "That's what we were wondering. And then we found another man-trap set not too far behind the cottage where Miss Anthea and Master David were when Lord Barrisford and I found them."

"Did you noticed anyone about who shouldn't be?" she asked, her eyes troubled.

"Two men—but not together," he answered. "One of them was Jack Downey, from The Golden Goose." He grinned at her shyly. "Could be he's just trying to improve the fare he offers at his suppers with a little pheasant. I've heard his food is none too good."

Meredith smiled back at him. "Who was the other one, Jack?"

"A tall man on horseback, miss. I've seen him going in to The Golden Goose—his name is Holt."

"Was he just riding past, though, Joe?" she inquired. "Perhaps he was just passing across our land."

Joe shook his head. "He had been into the spinney and got back upon his horse. When I went over to look, I found the man-trap only a few feet inside it."

"Well, it must surely have already been there and set," she observed. "A man on horseback couldn't carry such a thing. Some of them weigh as much as eighty pounds."

Joe nodded ruefully. "I know about that, miss. But I'll swear he knew about the trap and went in to look at it. He rode up on his horse, got off and walked straight in like he knew where he was going, and a minute or two later he was back on his horse and gone. I was going to come up to the Park tonight and tell Lord Barrisford about it."

"Thank you, Joe. I'll save you the trip—and I swear that we'll find who is doing this before someone else gets hurt."

"Aren't you going back to London, miss?" Joe asked tentatively.

Meredith paused in her plans, having momentarily forgotten all about the Dowager. "Oh yes—yes, I am, Joe," she replied almost regretfully. "I'll tell Lord Barrisford about it. He will have it taken out of the spinney and look into the matter, Joe."

She went directly to him in the library when she returned home.

"Another one?" Barrisford exclaimed. "Why on earth would anyone be doing such a thing?" he demanded.

Satisfied to see that he was as much at sea as she, Meredith replied smugly, "I'm sure that you'll look into the matter for us, Lord Barrisford, and settle it before someone is hurt."

"Like Joe was hurt, you mean?"

She glanced at him quickly. "Joe took a bad fall.

But I would hate to see him—or anyone else—come to grief on our property over such a matter as this."

Barrisford nodded grimly. "We can at least agree upon that much. And I would like to put my hands on the loose screw that's doing this."

"I'm certain that you will, Lord Barrisford," she replied coolly. "I will look forward to hearing how you have solved the problem."

"Ah yes, that's right, Miss Melville. It is my problem alone, is it not? You are returning to the pleasures of the city and leaving me here to deal with the problems at hand."

"I believe that you sent me a note telling me that there was no need for me to come down here despite the fact that both Thea and David had disappeared," she replied cooly. "You were quite confident that you could handle the matter—and you did find them. I feel certain that you will take care of this."

She paused at the door and looked back at him. "Of course, you had sent for the Runners, too. Thea's name was already a byword in the county, and now everyone in town knows that she was abducted by Sir Gerald and spent the night in his company. Most of them are unaware that he was locked up during that time."

Barrisford flushed and took a step toward her. "I realize that the Runner should not have been as free with his information as he was, but I was scarcely to blame for that."

Meredith looked at him in feigned surprise. "Oh, I wasn't blaming you, Lord Barrisford," she replied. "I was merely observing what happened. And you *did* return them safely, so I feel that I can trust you to take care of the man-traps and any other problems that might arise while I'm away."

"Now that I've committed myself to stay here as your guardian, you no longer feel the need to be agreeable, do you, Miss Merriville?" he asked, his tone cutting.

She smiled at him pleasantly. "If by that you mean that I no longer feel the need to throw myself at your feet in order to try to keep you here, then you would be correct, sir."

"And what if we need you here?" he demanded as she turned once again to the door. "Had you thought of that?"

She looked at him in genuine surprise this time. "Need me here? Who needs me, sir?"

"Your sister and brothers, of course," he replied somewhat weakly. He certainly could not bring himself to admit—either to her or himself—that he required her presence.

Meredith shook her head. "You mistake the matter. They are quite happy for the moment and, now that you have said that you will stay, I'm sure that David will do no more running away. Besides, you will be bringing them to your grandmother's for the holiday, and I will be with them then."

Barrisford watched her walk out the door with an unfamiliar pang. Even though he had scarcely spoken to her since her return, it was strange how great a difference her mere presence at Merton Park had meant to him. Despite the fact he had avoided her, he had known that she was nearby and that the chance turning of a corner might reveal her. Now she would be miles away and her thoughts, he was sure, would seldom be of him—not, of course, that that mattered, he had told himself hurriedly. It was merely the fact that she would be giving herself to having a good time while he was left caring for her family and her estate that bothered him.

"I suppose you'll be spending all of your time gadding about and thinking of no one but yourself!" he called after her.

"Precisely!" she called over her shoulder, not turning to look at him. "I take you as my model!"

She deliberately blocked all thought of what life would be like after Christmas was over and he took the children back to Merton Park. Barrisford was certainly not necessary to her happiness! She would simply take a leaf from his book and care for no one save herself and for nothing save her own happiness!

Barrisford sighed. He was about to be alone again with a houseful of children and a lunatic who persisted in setting traps for poachers and unwary passers-by. Just how this had happened to him evaded him.

Jeffries, of course, could have told him exactly how it had come to be. The valet assigned the blame to the diminutive redhead who could not be controlled, and he too watched with a sigh as Lady Barrisford's carriage rolled away, London-bound, while they continued in their rural retreat.

Eighteen

And Meredith was as good as her word. When she and Lady Barrisford returned to London, she threw herself into each activity with a feverish gaiety. No other young woman appeared to enjoy herself more than she. There were no further messages of kidnapping or disaster, and so she did not need to worry about those at Merton Park—nor about the man-traps.

A carelessly scrawled note from Evan even bore the comforting news that Joe was right: Jack Downey from The Golden Goose had indeed been setting the traps. He had been doing some poaching himself, and he wanted no one else cutting in on his territory. "Barrisford thinks that he hoped that I would fall into debt to him through my gambling there, and that he would thus have a hold on me so that he could continue raiding our land to try to improve his blasted suppers," Evan wrote. He had added smugly, "We were too canny for him by half, though. He won't catch me in such a snare as that."

Edmund Adams had awaited her return eagerly, and had served as her escort to a number of evening parties. Lady Barrisford was cautious, however. She made certain that other young men were also in Meredith's company so that Adams' attentions could not grow too particular.

Meredith thought often of Lord Barrisford, however, more often than she cared to admit even to herself. Each time that Adams said something charming or did something particularly thoughtful, she found herself thinking that Barrisford would never say or do such a thing. Then, annoyed that she was bothering to think of him at all, she would give her full attention to the matter at hand, determined to drive out any thought of him at all.

One evening a few weeks after her return, she found herself singled out at an evening party by a very handsome woman who introduced herself as Maria Danvers.

"You are the young lady who is the ward of Lord Barrisford, are you not?" she inquired, seating herself next to Meredith while Edmund had gone in search of refreshment for them.

Meredith looked at her in some surprise. She had not been introducing herself in such a manner, but simply as a guest of Lady Barrisford.

Mrs. Danvers saw her expression and laughed. "Don't be put off by me, my dear. I do my best to keep up with Barrisford, so I know very well who you are, Miss Melville."

Meredith inclined her head and mouthed the appropriate response, looking curiously at the lady.

"Forgive me for asking, Miss Danvers, but why do

you try to keep up with Lord Barrisford?" she inquired. "Are you old friends?"

Mrs. Danvers laughed again. "It is Mrs. Danvers, my dear. I have been married for twenty years—and that is exactly why I try to keep up with Barrisford. He and I were . . . very close a few years ago. I must have some pleasure in life, so when he is in London, I look forward to seeing him."

She leaned close to Meredith before rising to depart. "And I assure you that I'm not the only one, my dear. You are most fortunate in your guardian. I wish you well."

Meredith regarded her with distaste as she rejoined her own party. So this was one of Barrisford's array of married lovers. She had heard that he had had many—all beautiful, all intelligent, and all amusing. It was no wonder he had not found her interesting, she thought, watching Mrs. Danvers across the room as she flirted gracefully and danced with a handsome man. And it was no wonder that he resented being forced to keep a gaggle of children in some rural retreat.

Well, let him resent it, she thought angrily, still watching the radiant Mrs. Danvers. She had done it for long enough. And Lord Barrisford was not the only one that deserved a life.

When Edmund returned with a plate of delicacies and a glass of champagne for her, he discovered to his delight that Meredith was in a most flirtatious mood. The evening ended less happily, however, for Meredith turned to him in the carriage during the ride home and asked him a question, her tone serious.

"Do you think a married lady must remain faithfu to her husband?" she demanded.

"It would depend, I suppose, upon whether or no we were speaking of my wife or someone else's," h responded lightly. Seeing her expression, howeve he quickly erased all trace of amusement from voic and face.

"Anyone's!" she replied sharply.

"Yes, I suppose so," he said reluctantly becoming serious. "It doesn't always work that way, though, yo know—"

"And do you think that having an affair with a mar ried woman is right?" she demanded. "Have you ha such a relationship, Mr. Adams?"

Edmund flushed deeply. "That isn't the sort o thing that a gentleman discusses, Miss Melville," h said reprovingly. "Nor a young lady."

"Well, you must forgive me, sir," she said stiffly. " am from the country, you see, and we apparently liv by a different code than you gentlemen do in the city.

Before Edmund could discuss it further, they ha arrived in Grosvenor Square and he was escorting her to the door, where she made it abundantly clea that she would brook no more discussion.

Perhaps it was true that all gentlemen were lik Lord Barrisford, she thought grimly, as she brushe her hair and prepared for bed that night. Perhap he was even better than most because he made n pretense of being other than he was.

She was not particularly surprised—nor particu larly interested—when Edmund Adams appeared a early the next day as propriety allowed. His huge bou

quet of hothouse roses had already arrived, bearing
a note of apology and asking her to attend the ballet
with him the next evening. Meredith accepted—but
without enthusiasm—and it soon became apparent
both to him and to the Dowager that something was
seriously amiss.

To Adams she would admit nothing, but with Lady
Barrisford she was more forthcoming. Indeed, that
lady left her little choice.

"Come now, child," she said that evening as they
returned from a concert. "Tell me what's wrong. Are
you not feeling well?"

"I am quite well, thank you, ma'am," Meredith replied quietly, seating herself and preparing for the
inquisition that she had been expecting.

"Well, then, what's to do?" demanded Lady Barrisford. "You are not acting like yourself at all!"

"Am I not?" inquired Meredith absently. "How am
different?"

"Precisely in the way that you answered me just now.
It's not that you don't talk—but when you do, you
don't sound like yourself. You sound as though you
are miles away—and you walk like a person in a
dream."

"Yes, I suppose I do," agreed Meredith in the same
faraway tone. "Please forgive me, ma'am. It isn't that
I don't appreciate everything that you are doing for
me."

The Dowager tapped her fingernail so sharply
against the table next to her that Meredith jumped
a little. "It's not appreciation that I want, my dear! I

want you to enjoy yourself as you were before. Wha
has happened to change all of that?"

Meredith paused a moment, then forced herself t
reply. "I don't have anyone to talk to about thi
ma'am, since I have no mother or older female rela
tive, so perhaps you won't mind if I talk to you," sh
began tentatively.

"Not at all," said the Dowager encouragingly. "Tel
me quite frankly what it is that's troubling you."

"Do all married ladies and gentlemen have af
fairs?" Meredith asked baldly. "Is that something tha
I must simply expect if I marry?"

Somewhat taken aback, Lady Barrisford scrutinize
her for a moment. "Not all of 'em, my dear—but ;
good many," she responded frankly. "Are you think
ing of someone in particular?"

Meredith nodded. "Mr. Adams," she responded.

"Well, of course he's never been married, so it'
hard to say—" Here the Dowager broke off an
stared at her intently until Meredith was forced t
look up. "Come, come, my girl," she said encourag
ingly. "What brought all of this on?"

Meredith hesitated a moment. "Well, I was ap
proached yesterday evening by a Mrs. Maria Danvers,"
she began, and Lady Barrisford nodded sharply.

"Maria Danvers!" she exclaimed. "I might have ex
pected something like this to happen. She was talking
about my grandson, wasn't she?"

Meredith nodded. "And I knew, of course, abou
Lord Barrisford's reputation, but I hadn't reall'
thought about what it meant. And when I asked M

Adams if he had ever had an affair with a married lady, he wouldn't answer me directly."

"Well, naturally he wouldn't," said Lady Barrisford briskly. "That would scarcely be the part of a gentleman. He isn't expected to brag about his conquests—nor is a lady."

"So I gathered," responded Meredith drily. "It's just that it seemed to me that it wasn't the part of a gentleman or a lady to behave in such a manner to begin with—but then I realize that I have been all my life in the country."

"Things are different in London," Lady Barrisford conceded, "but they're somewhat different than you think them in the country as well. You must remember, my dear, that you have been living the life of a child."

Meredith nodded dully. "I know that now. That is why I decided that I must talk to you. If this is something that I must accept, then I shall do so."

Lady Barrisford vigorously cursed Maria Danvers and her grandson to herself, then forced herself to speak gently. "Miss Melville, when you marry, you will be marrying a man with faults, no matter how perfect he may seem—so it may well be that you have to bear with his indiscretions."

"I see," responded Meredith in a low voice.

"But I will tell you, my dear," added the Dowager, "that my late husband was faithful to me and I to him until the day of his death—and insofar as I ever heard, that was true of your mother and father as well."

She was comforted to see Meredith's face brighten as she said this. "So you must not think that affairs are a requirement of marriage—but it is as well not to go into marriage blindly, and to know that this is a possibility."

"Thank you, ma'am," said Meredith simply. "It makes me happy to know that some have lived in the manner that seems proper and desirable to me—even if there are men like—even if there are men who are more interested in their own needs than in those of the people they love."

Lady Barrisford watched her thoughtfully as she rose and left the room. Devlin had made a mull of this, indulging himself as the lover of married women. And now Edmund Adams, whom she had hoped to use to prod her grandson into action, looked as though he might be a serious contender for Meredith's interests. She tried to force herself to acknowledge that things might not turn out as she wished, but she was unable to do so.

She was quite determined to have Meredith as her granddaughter despite the efforts of Maria Danvers and Edmund Adams.

Nineteen

The party from Merton Park arrived for Christmas soon after Lady Barrisford and Meredith had their talk. The conversation seemed to have restored the girl to her normal good spirits, mused the Dowager. At any rate, she was once again lively and apparently happy. And, to the Dowager's relief, when Edmund Adams attempted to grow more particular in his attentions, Meredith lightly sidestepped them, sharing her favors among a group of amusing young men.

Lord Barrisford and his group arrived later in the day than they had planned, and he discovered to his chagrin that Miss Melville had already gone out for the evening. He had not allowed himself to recognize how much he had looked forward to seeing her, but his grandmother was pleased to note that his mood was exceedingly cross after he realized that she had already left.

"I daresay that you might join them if you hurried, Devlin," said the Dowager, enjoying his discomfort. "You know that Mrs. Ingram would have invited you had she expected you here in time."

"I'm surprised that Miss Melville cared so little

about welcoming her family to London that she would go out on the very evening they were expected," he observed stiffly, carefully excluding himself when speaking of the family.

"Well, Devlin, we expected you by mid-afternoon, you know. And she had accepted this invitation some time before you had let us know the precise date of your arrival."

She leaned over and patted his hand. "Besides, as you can see, the children were exhausted by their trip and have already taken themselves off to bed. Meredith was quite sure that was the way it would be."

"So it is Meredith now instead of Miss Melville," said Barrisford. "You two must be getting on well together."

"Well enough," acknowledged his grandmother. "I have grown very partial to the child."

"Perhaps because she doesn't crack you over the head with a vase," he said tartly.

"Perhaps because I don't attempt to call the tune for her to dance to," returned the Dowager. "And despite the fact that I referred to her as a child, I know that she is not one."

Devlin rose and paced up and down the room, ruffling his hair as he walked. "Aren't you giving her too much liberty?" he asked abruptly. "Why aren't you with her tonight?"

"There was no need," replied the Dowager placidly. "I know the two young men who have escorted her and I know Mrs. Ingram—so I chose to stay at home so that I could welcome all of you."

"Very thoughtful, I'm sure," said Barrisford, still

pacing, "but it may be that she is younger than you think and needs more guidance than you presently think necessary."

"Devlin, do sit down!" snapped his grandmother. "You're making me tired, both with your pacing and your manner. Whoever told you that you should try to run this poor child's life merely because you chanced to be appointed her guardian?"

"She is my responsibility," he said stiffly.

"So she is," agreed the Dowager. "Something that you failed to remember when you kissed her. And yet here you are, complaining because she has gone out to the home of one of my friends with two young men who watch each other's every move like jealous dogs with a single bone. What could be safer?"

"Well, you may be right," he admitted unwillingly. "Still, I would feel better if she were here now and I knew that all was well with her."

"Yes, I'm sure that would make you feel better," said his grandmother comfortably, "but she isn't here, and so you will have to wait until later in the evening to feel that way. In the meantime, we shall think of Meredith and allow her to be happy—something that she hasn't been for quite a long time."

"What does that mean?" he demanded, staring into his grandmother's eyes.

"Just what I said," she responded. "Meredith hasn't felt contented for quite a long time. Why should she not have a little time of her own now?"

He grudgingly acknowledged that this might be in order, and took himself away to his chamber to change for Mrs. Ingram's evening party. Jeffries, informed of his master's intentions, watched him warily as he laid out his clothes and helped him dress.

"And so Miss Melville is already there?" asked Jeffries casually as he masterfully arranged Barrisford's crisp white neckcloth into a veritable cascade of linen.

"Yes," replied Barrisford briefly, giving his valet no encouragement.

Jeffries, however, required none. "I suppose it will be nice for you to be at a London party again after all these weeks of ruralizing," he continued. "I don't blame you for rushing off the instant you have the opportunity to do so."

Barrisford snorted. "One of Sarah Ingram's parties is about as exciting as a late afternoon nap!"

"Well, then of course I understand why you are impatient to go," returned Jeffries, probing gently.

Barrisford looked sharply at him, and the conversation lapsed. As Barrisford left his chamber, however, Jeffries looked after him thoughtfully. His master might not know just why he was attending the evening party, but his valet was all too keenly aware of the reason.

When Barrisford arrived at Mrs. Ingram's home on Half-Moon Street, that lady was delighted to welcome him, assuring him again and again that he needed no formal invitation to come to see her. It was with considerable satisfaction that she led him into the company rooms herself to display him to her other guests.

"Look who has joined us unexpectedly, Alvord," she chirped to her husband, towing her prize alongside her.

"It's good to see you, Barrisford," returned Mr. Ingram, leaving his card game for a moment. "Would you care to join us?"

"Not just now," he responded. "Perhaps a little later in the evening."

Nodding, Mr. Ingram rejoined his group and the game continued. After a few more minutes, Barrisford managed to escape his hostess and look for Miss Melville himself.

When he found her, he was somewhat less than charmed by her situation. She was being entertained by two very youthful companions who were clearly smitten by her. He watched unseen for a moment, thinking disdainfully what puppies the two young men were and how easily she was amused.

"Good evening, Miss Melville," he finally said coolly. "How delightful to see you again."

Startled, Meredith glanced up quickly. "Why, Lord Barrisford!" she exclaimed. "I didn't expect to see you here tonight."

"I daresay you did not," he replied, smiling and bowing. "Still I thought that perhaps I should be here to escort you home."

"There will be no need of that," she assured him, indicating the two young men at hand. "Mr. Samuels and Mr. Jameson are willing to see me home."

"We are looking forward to doing so," agreed Mr. Samuels, and Mr Jameson nodded in agreement.

"As you wish," said Lord Barrisford, turning abruptly and leaving them without further conversation.

"What a very strange man," remarked Mr. Samuels, looking after him, and Mr. Jameson once again nodded his agreement.

"He is most certainly that," said Meredith impatiently, wishing that he would keep his distance and allow her to enjoy herself. His sudden appearance had taken the shine from the evening, and she was hard pressed to continue giving her undivided attention to the two eager young men who were dogging her every step.

As though he had read her mind, Lord Barrisford kept a considerable distance between himself and Meredith for the next few days. Despite the fact that they were all together several times, attending the theatre and taking Thea shopping and riding in the Park, he kept himself apart from her, concentrating his attention on the other three.

David went with them everywhere, taking it all in with wide eyes, but still never speaking. Even when they went to the Surrey to see The Blood Red Knight, a handsome roan horse, perform, followed by a series of acts and a pantomime, he remained unmoved, although watching everything from dark, shining eyes.

To his great delight, on Christmas Eve morning he found a great heap of holly and ivy at the foot of the stairs when he came down to breakfast.

"I'm glad that you're pleased, David," said the Dowager, watching his expression. "Merry told me that you have always loved the tradition of decorating the house with greens before Christmas. Would you like to do that for me?"

David nodded eagerly, glancing up the steps toward Evan, who was warbling a cheerful little tune about a pretty, dark-eyed girl and carefully smoothing the linen of his nattily tied cravat.

Seeing the greens, he momentarily lost his sophistication and swooped down upon them.

"The holly and ivy!" he exclaimed jubilantly. "Come along, Merry! We have work to do! And where's Thea? She's the one who must make the kissing bough!"

"The kissing bough?" inquired the Dowager with raised eyebrows. "And where do you plan to place that, sir?"

"Right over your head, ma'am," responded Evan impudently, holding a sprig of mistletoe over her head and kissing her on the cheek.

Pleased as always by a saucy young man, the Dowager smiled and waved him away. "I take no responsibility for what comes of it," she announced, returning to the breakfast table. "I don't see how Merry has been able to keep up with you for all of these years."

"I haven't," responded Meredith lightly.

She had been waiting on the landing, watching David's reaction. Pleased by Evan's exuberant enthusiasm, even though she was certain that he had his own plans for that kissing bough, she allowed herself to be swept into the fury of activity that ensued. No corner of the house was safe from the cascade of greenery.

Thea labored for hours over a delightful confection of interlacing hoops of holly and ivy studded with bright oranges and apples, bows of scarlet ribbon, delicate paper roses. From the bough hung a single bunch of mistletoe.

"It is a work of art, Thea," announced Lord Barrisford in admiration, taking it from her to hang over the entryway to the drawing room. "And a dangerous one. You have now placed everyone in the household in peril. No one going through this doorway will be safe."

Thea blushed prettily as he bent over to kiss her lightly on the cheek, for she had come too close to it as she watched him adjust the bough.

"Here, here! That will be enough of that!" announced Evan in a fierce, fatherly voice, fully an octave deeper than his normal tone. "You young people have to be watched at every turn!"

Thea giggled. "You sound just like Colonel Pitt, Evan! He is forever saying that to us! Do it again!"

Evan cheerfully complied and Thea once again dissolved in laughter while David watched them, smiling.

"You're very quiet, ma'am," observed Barrisford to Merry, who was watching them from her perch on a nearby ladder. "Is there anything wrong?"

She shook her head. "Nothing at all. I'm just glad to see them happy—even if it's only for a few minutes." She turned her gaze from them to Barrisford. "It's very kind of you and your grandmother to do this for us."

Caught off guard by the simple sincerity of her remark, he stared at her for a moment, then smiled. "Perhaps you haven't noticed it, Miss Melville, bu you—and the rest of your family—appear to be giving my grandmother a great deal of pleasure."

And Meredith knew that he was speaking the truth. She and the Dowager had gotten on very well together, but her hostess also enjoyed her banter with Evan and Thea's beauty—and she knew that David's plight had touched the old lady, too.

"I'm glad of it," she replied. "It is a pity that we don't give you the same degree of pleasure, sir." In saying this, she carefully averted her gaze to the romping of the others and avoided his eyes.

Barrisford would not allow this, however, for he cupped his hand under her chin and turned her face toward his.

"And how do you know that you haven't, Miss Melville?" he inquired, his eyes warm upon her.

"You would not have been thinking of leaving us if that were so," she replied. "Why would you leave what gives you pleasure?"

"Perhaps because I am afraid. Had you thought of that?"

Meredith looked at him skeptically, determined not to be taken in by the dark invitation of his eyes. "No," she said frankly. "I cannot imagine you afraid of anything, sir—least of all, of us."

"I am afraid only of you, Miss Melville—only of you."

Meredith jerked her head back, removing her chin from the warmth of his hand. "I am not one of your flirts, sir! I do wish that you would remember not to practice your lines upon me!"

Before he could reply to this, Thea began to sing,

and the rest of them grew silent. She had a lovely voice, tender and well suited to the old tune that she was singing. The words seemed to float through the air, taking on a life of their own, and Meredith listened to each one as though she had never heard it before.

> *As the holly groweth green*
> *And never changeth hue,*
> *So am I, ever hath been,*
> *To my lady true.*
>
> *As the holly groweth green*
> *With ivy all alone,*
> *When flower cannot be seen,*
> *And greenwood leaves be gone.*
>
> *Now unto my lady*
> *Promise to her I make,*
> *From all others only*
> *To her I me betake.*

"How wonderful it would be to have a lover who would write such a thing!" sighed Thea as she finished.

Glancing at Barrisford, her sister retorted sharply, "Yes, Henry VIII was precisely the sort of man you would expect to say such nonsense! We all know how true he was to *each* of his ladies! What folly to listen to honeyed words when the speaker has no heart!"

"It's still a lovely piece, Merry!" pouted Thea. "Someday I want someone to write such a thing for me—and to mean it!"

"Now that is the trick, my dear—being certain that he means it," responded Meredith, looking away from Barrisford and trying to speak more lightly. "Ah, well—as lovely as you are, Thea, I have no doubt that someday it will happen."

"Yes, well, my fear is that it will happen far too many times," chimed in Evan, "and that you will believe each and every one of them."

He wisely took to his heels as soon as he had said this, for Thea reached for the scissors she had been using in her construction of the bough and, threatening to cut off one of his lovely locks of hair to add to its decoration, raced after him, David on her heels.

Taking advantage of the confusion, Meredith slipped from the room, leaving Barrisford alone.

That night the Dowager oversaw the lighting of the Yule log. "An old-fashioned custom, I know," she admitted, "but my father and grandfather did it, and I still enjoy it."

So did the children, who crowded around to watch it being lighted.

"Now we must be very careful not to let it go out," she cautioned, "or we will bring bad luck upon the house." The rest of them smiled at the old-fashioned notion, but David nodded seriously, and he made it his business to keep a close eye upon the fire.

"This little marble hearth is certainly not as majestic as the huge brick one in the Hall at Sutherland," said Lady Barrisford, "but it will do for the moment." She cast a sidelong look at her grandson. "Perhaps before I die, I will see Devlin settled at Sutherland with his own family, and be present to see them light the Yule log there once more."

Her undutiful grandson glared at her and turned away from the fire.

Evan, however, was looking at her guiltily. "And we're the ones responsible for keeping him away from Sutherland, aren't we, Lady Barrisford?" he asked. "I hadn't considered the fact that we could be keeping him from settling and having a family of his own."

"You're not, Evan," said Barrisford shortly. "You may believe me when I say there is nothing farther from my mind than marriage."

Evan brightened a little at that. "Well, then we might as well enjoy ourselves, hadn't we?"

Managing to get Barrisford a little apart from the others, he said in a low voice, "Do you suppose that while we're here, sir, you might take me to one of the hells and show me how things are done here?"

Barrisford looked at him with amusement, although he tried as best he could to disguise it. "I'm afraid, Evan, that you need to be a little older to attend any of the gaming establishments that I frequent in London," he said gently. "It isn't quite like The Golden Goose at home."

Evan, his cheeks self-consciously pink, responded, "Well, of course I realize that it isn't at all the same, sir. That's why I wished for you to show me just—"

"When you are a little older, Evan," he said. "After you've been a year or two at Oxford, I'll take you with me for an evening and show you a different side of London."

As Barrisford had expected, Evan looked dejected
for a day or two and moped about, but soon brightened up again. Unfortunately, so absorbed was he in
his own thoughts that he did not keep quite such
careful track of the boy as he had at first. Once or
twice Evan disappeared early in the evening, and
when Meredith questioned him about his whereabouts, he shrugged it off, saying that he had merely
been strolling about, seeing what a big city looked
like after dark. Since he spent most of his time with
them, no one thought too much about it, being too
caught up in their own activities to notice.

It was at a delightful Christmas ball two nights before
the end of their visit that Barrisford and Meredith
once again came to grief. His grandmother was exhausted after an excursion to the Park that afternoon,
and she delegated him to escort Meredith to the ball
that night. He did precisely that, maintaining a cool,
distant conversation with her in the carriage, and making no attempt to dance with anyone himself. Instead,
he watched from the side, not even retiring into one
of the cardrooms to entertain himself. He looked,
Meredith thought, like some messenger of doom, hov-
ering to choose his victim. He scarcely smiled once
during the course of the evening.

It was late in the evening when she came to grief.
She had been dancing with a young man she had
met a few days earlier; he unfortunately fancied himself as a ladies' man, holding her altogether too close
during the waltz. Before she could extricate herself
from his warm embrace, she was looking into the icy

eyes of Lord Barrisford, who ruthlessly cut in on them, sending the young man about his business.

"You waltz well, sir," she said at last, when it appeared there would be no conversation at all, "but then I would have expected as much."

"You need to be more careful, Miss Melville," he said coldly. "Why did you allow that young man to hold you so closely? Don't you know that your reputation can be ruined in the twinkling of an eye?"

"If you were paying attention, Lord Barrisford," she returned, "I believe you will have noticed that I tried to disengage myself, but he would not let me go. Short of creating a scene on the dance floor—which definitely *would* have drawn attention to my situation and possibly placing my reputation at risk—I decided to finish the dance."

At the end of the dance he informed her that they would be returning home, despite the fact that there were several dances and the supper left to enjoy. She glanced at his expression and did not argue—for the moment. Once in the privacy of their carriage, however, she felt no such discretion was necessary.

"And why, sir, may I ask, did you think it necessary to drag me from the ball before I was ready to leave?" she asked.

"I think it should be obvious, Miss Melville," he responded coolly.

"I'm afraid that it isn't at all obvious to me, Lord Barrisford. Do explain it for me."

"Very well," he responded. "You were not being circumspect in your behavior. I would imagine that my grandmother, being old, has indulged you too much and allowed you to run wild."

"To run wild?" gasped Meredith indignantly. "Lord Barrisford, you are not talking to some schoolgirl with no common sense! I know very well there was no need to remove me from that ball except for your need to control everyone else's actions—particularly mine!"

"You are wrong!" he said indignantly. "This was for your own good. If you won't think about your reputation, I must do so."

She laughed bitterly. "Just like you thought about Maria Danvers' reputation?" she inquired. "And did you think about her husband's reputation?"

Catching a glimpse of his face, she laughed again. "I thought not," she said with satisfaction.

"Who told you about Maria Danvers?" he demanded.

"She did," responded Meredith shortly. "And so I can scarcely see, sir, just how you are able in good conscience to criticize me for allowing myself to be held a little too close when your own actions have been much worthier of criticism." She turned to look at him. "I can understand, however, why you find us such dull company at Merton Park—and why you find me so uninteresting since you have loved women like Maria Danvers."

For a moment Barrisford could not trust himself to reply. Then, suddenly so intensely aware of her presence next to him that he could scarcely bear it, he turned and swept her into his arms.

He had expected her to resist. He knew there was

no vase handy, but he expected at the least to have his ears boxed—but to his amazed delight, Meredith seemed to melt in his arms. There was no resistance; instead, there was a passionate response to his kiss. Small though she was, he seemed to find himself being absorbed by her. Meredith's arms about his neck pulled him down to her, and he buried his face in the tenderness of her neck and bosom.

"I didn't love them," he whispered. "I never loved them—"

For a few moments they both forgot where they were, but as the carriage slowed, they scarcely had time to rearrange themselves before the door opened and a footman appeared to help them down.

They were silent, not even glancing at one another as they walked up the stairs toward their chambers. When they reached her door, Lord Barrisford bowed briefly.

"Thank you for a delightful evening, Miss Melville," he said in a low voice. And he had put out his hand to pull her toward him, when he heard someone clear her throat behind him.

"I beg your pardon, Lord Barrisford," said Thayer, his grandmother's maid, bobbing a nervous curtsey, "but her Ladyship asks that you both stop in her chamber before you retire for the evening."

The pair of them turned and walked to the Dowager's chamber like two being led to the gallows. Very aware of the maid's presence, Meredith could not do anything about her tumbled curls nor her flushed cheeks, and Barrisford was all too aware of the wreckage of his immaculate cravat.

Nor did the Dowager's hawk-like gaze miss a detail. Smiling at Meredith, she said gently, "Run along, child. You need your rest for tomorrow."

Gratefully, Meredith hurried toward the door, abandoning Barrisford to his fate.

"Come here, Devlin," said his grandmother, beckoning him to her side from her nest of snowy pillows. Reluctantly, he approached her side and sat down on the edge of the bed as she indicated.

"Just what have you been doing, Devlin?" she asked, plucking a long red-gold hair from his jacket.

Feeling as though he were sixteen years old again, Barrisford flushed to the roots of his hair. But he did not answer, having no adequate response.

Looking at his face, she nodded. "I thought as much. I had considered letting Meredith go back to Merton Park with you when you return, because I know, though she says nothing about it, that from time to time she is a little homesick. I see by this, though, that I cannot send her with you."

She stared at him a minute more. "Devlin, how could you take advantage of a young woman whose well-being rests in your hands? She has no one except me to turn to."

"I didn't—as you do delicately put it—take advantage of her," he returned, and then he stopped. He could scarcely say that Meredith had returned his kisses, for that merely made everything worse. All he could do was to lapse into silence.

His grandmother waited for a moment, then dismissed him with a wave of her hand, saying in a tired voice, "See to it that you aren't left alone with the child, Devlin. It is the least that you can do for all of us."

And as he quietly left the room and closed the door behind him, the Dowager smiled. Things were going quite as well as she had hoped, and it was clear that each of them was attracted to the other.

The Dowager saw to it that the two remaining days were spent in a whirl of activity. Everyone enjoyed going to Covent Garden to see the great Grimaldi in *The Golden Egg,* all of them charmed by his antics and his white face and scarlet half-mooned cheeks.

"Well, this has been delightful," observed Meredith as the show ended. "In fact, all of your visit has been a pleasure. I shall hate to see you all return to Merton Park tomorrow."

"Aren't you coming back with us, Merry?" asked Thea. "We had thought that you were."

"I suppose you're having too good a time, Merry, making too many conquests to be bothered with coming home with us," remarked Evan, laughing.

For a moment Meredith was sorely tempted to say that she would return with them, but before she could speak, Lady Barrisford intervened.

"I am afraid that she cannot come just yet, Evan. She has accepted a good many invitations that it would be awkward to refuse now. Meredith will come home soon enough—or perhaps all of you will come again to visit me."

This comment created the diversion she had hoped for, as they all fell into remembering the good times they had had during their visit and discussing possible outings for a new visit.

It was with some pain that Meredith watched her family depart the next day. She had to admit to herself that she was going to miss not only them, but also Lord Barrisford. He had made it quite clear, however, that he had regretted his indiscretion and he had kept a cool and unmistakable distance between them at all times, never even accidentally catching her eye.

She wiped a tear from her eye as she watched them leave. She was homesick, but now she had no home. She could not go home again to Merton Park because Lord Barrisford would be there—and she couldn't bear to live so closely with him and yet feel the distance between them. She sighed. Nor could she impose forever upon the Dowager's hospitality.

She stared out the window as she came to her decision. She really had no other choice. She must marry. And her choice was really quite an easy one. Edmund Adams was an attractive, amiable man and he had already made his intentions known. If she married him, she would have an establishment of her own, and she could at least have her family come to visit her. She would accept him.

Twenty

Having made up her mind to accept Edmund Adams, Meredith allowed herself to return to her round of routs and balls and breakfasts, telling herself that soon she would slow down and allow him to approach Lady Barrisford about the marriage. First, she told herself, she needed to remove all thought of Lord Barrisford from her mind—and that would require activity. Unfortunately, after two weeks of feverish gaiety, she still saw him at every turn and heard his voice whenever Edmund tried to talk to her and felt his arms about her when she lay down to go to sleep. And so she delayed.

Finally, however, Edmund caught her alone and proposed to her. Having already practiced her acceptance speech, she was able to deliver it quite flawlessly, and Edmund repaired to the Dowager to ask her permission for the marriage.

"I'm afraid, Mr. Adams, that it is to my grandson that you should be appealing. He is the legal guardian of the Melvilles," she told him.

"I beg your pardon, Lady Barrisford," he said. "I had thought that you had the authority to make such decisions since Miss Melville has taken up residence with you."

The Dowager shook her head firmly. "Devlin is very jealous of his prerogatives," she said. "I would not wish to anger him by overstepping my rights."

"Of course not," agreed Mr. Adams, "and I wish to be certain that I do have permission to marry Miss Melville, particularly since she is quite young. I shall go to Merton Park immediately."

"Very wise," agreed the Dowager. "I would suggest that you write to Devlin rather than go to see him, however. A letter would give him time to think everything over."

"Very true," said Mr. Adams. "I do appreciate your help, Lady Barrisford," he said politely, bowing to her.

"It has been my pleasure," she responded affably, thinking to herself that she would give much to see Devlin's face when he read that letter.

Mr. Adams dispatched his letter with alacrity, and eagerly awaited the reply.

It was only two nights later that Meredith was in her chamber, preparing for yet another ball, when a maid came to inform her she had a caller in the library.

Slipping hurriedly into a walking dress, Meredith ran lightly down the steps. This was not the time for callers, so she was certain that something out of the way was happening. To her shock, when she opened the library door, she saw Joe Walters standing awkwardly in the middle of the room, his hat in his hand, trying to stay away from all of the furniture and to stand as lightly as possible on the thick carpeting.

"Joe!" she exclaimed, coming forward with her

hand outstretched. "How good to see you!" Then, looking at his expression, she stopped. "Is there something wrong?" she asked fearfully. "Has David run away again?"

To her relief, he shook his head. "No, Miss Melville," he assured her. "David's fine, but it's because of him that I've come." He dug about for a moment in his pocket, then brought forth a much-folded piece of paper that he tried vainly to smooth before handing it to her.

"David wrote this," he explained, "and asked me to bring it to you." Here he pointed to capital letters spelling out her name on the outside of the folded paper.

"Do sit down, Joe," she said, motioning to one of the nearby chairs. "Let me see what he has to say that is so important."

She grew pale as she read his note. "It's Evan," she explained, not looking up. "He's been slipping out at night to go to The Golden Goose again and David has been following him." She paused a moment and looked up. "Where is Lord Barrisford while all of this is going on? Why hasn't he put a stop to it?" she demanded.

"He's been gone a week or so to his own home," explained Joe. "He received a message from Sutherland saying there was an emergency there."

Meredith stood up abruptly as she finished reading the note. "David says that Evan's lost money gambling again and he can't pay his debts—and that he has been cleaning and oiling a pair of pistols. What on earth can Evan be thinking of doing?" she demanded.

Joe stared at her as she ran to the door. "Do wait for me, Joe. I must go up and see Lady Barrisford immediately."

Meredith explained her problem to the astonished Dowager, who agreed that she should set out for Merton Park with all possible haste.

"I will have my carriage prepared for you immediately and send Thayer and the young man who came with the letter back with you tonight. You can travel as far as John Coachman thinks advisable tonight and set out again at daylight tomorrow. I will hire a postchaise and follow you as soon as possible."

"Thank you, Lady Barrisford!" she exclaimed, throwing her arms around the old woman's neck. "I hope that I'm in time to keep Evan from doing something foolish."

"So do I, child," she responded, pleased with the mark of affection. "I will send a note to Sutherland to notify Devlin of what is happening so that he may join you as soon as possible and take care of the problem before anything unfortunate happens."

The Dowager was as good as her word, and Meredith, accompanied by Thayer and Joe, set forth for Merton Park within the hour. A note was also dispatched to Barrisford at Sutherland so that he could also take himself there with all possible speed. Lady Barrisford nodded to herself as she wrote it. Once he knew that Evan was in trouble and Meredith was returning, she had no doubt that her grandson would reach Merton Park with remarkable speed.

* * *

David had been quite accurate in his observations. As soon as Barrisford had left for Sutherland, Evan had once again taken up his evenings at The Golden Goose. While in London, Evan had slipped out on two different occasions to one of the forbidden hells. He had fallen into conversation with another young man while riding in the Park and had confided his desire to visit such a place. To his delight, Mr. Harrell had offered to be his escort. On the first night he had won, but on the second evening he had lost a quite significant amount. He had managed to pay his debt only by adjourning to a pawnshop and selling his gold watch.

He had been surprised but pleased to receive a note from Mr. Harrell, announcing that he had decided to break his journey at The Goose and asking Evan to join him for an evening of play. It seemed to him that his luck was entirely out, for he lost at everything he tried. Although he was careful to avoid playing with Mr. Holt, he still lost money at a far more rapid rate than he ever had before. It was, in fact, beginning to look quite desperate. Mr. Harrell would be leaving the next day, and Evan had no money with which to pay his very sizable debt of honor.

"Three thousand pounds!" exclaimed young Findlay, a friend of Evan's in whom he had decided to confide. His eyes were almost starting from his head as he stared at Evan. "How could you have lost so much in just three nights, Melville?"

Evan, who had been wondering much the same thing himself, shrugged. "I guess my luck was out," he said, trying to strike a casual pose.

"I guess your wits were out," retorted his friend. "After you lost one thousand, why didn't you give it up? Why did you go back for two more nights?"

"Everyone knows," explained Evan patiently, "that if you keep playing, you eventually have a streak of luck."

Findlay snorted. "If you keep playing and losing, you eventually have no money and no home!"

Evan flushed a little, for Mr. Harrell had indeed mentioned the possibility of accepting Evan's horse—or his ring—or an interest in Merton Park as his payment. It was then that the full horror of what was happening had begun to weigh upon him, and he had cast about for a solution to his problem.

If Barrisford had been at home, he might have confided in him, but as it was, he decided that he would have to solve his own problem. And his solution was most unusual. Carefully he explained it to his friend, and Findlay's eyes grew even wider.

"Why, that's highway robbery, Melville!" he exclaimed, horrified. "You can't do that!"

"No, you're quite right that I can't do it alone," Evan conceded. "I will need your help. That's why I'm telling you about all of this."

"Need *my* help?" exclaimed the unfortunate Findlay. "To do what?"

"To help me rob the coach," he explained patiently.

"What?" shrieked his friend.

After Findlay had grown relatively calm once more, Evan again explained to him his urgent need for money.

"But this is the height of idiocy," insisted Findlay, "and besides that, old boy, what is so very wonderful about taking money from people to repay a debt of honor? How is taking someone else's money to repay a debt the honorable thing to do? Seems to me that there's something a bit off about that line of thinking."

"Well, of course there is, you ass!" snapped Evan. "If I could think of anything else to do, I would do it, wouldn't I? And I'll get the names of the people and send them the money as soon as I have it."

Findlay stared at him. "Do you mean to say that you're going to repay the people you rob?" he demanded.

"Of course I am! I'm no thief! Now are you with me or not?"

Findlay nodded, falling into a meditative silence at this newest development. He couldn't very well let Evan go alone and get himself shot, and now that they would be repaying their victims, he could accept the robbery itself more gracefully.

By the time they had arranged their costumes and their procedure for the robbery and gotten themselves to the proper bend in the road, they discovered that they had missed the stagecoach.

"Well, no matter," said Evan cheerfully. "Someone will be along in a little while and we'll stop them."

They had only a thirty-minute wait before a dark coach slowed and rolled around the corner where they waited in the middle of the road, pistols drawn and loaded. As the coach drew uncertainly to a stop to avoid hitting them, Evan called out, "Stand and deliver!"

Dropping his voice, he whispered to Findlay, "I've always wanted to say that."

"What's going on out there?" demanded a voice from within the carriage. "Why have we stopped, coachman?"

"We're being robbed, ma'am," he replied. "Just keep your seat in the carriage."

"Being robbed!" exclaimed the voice. "Let me see these bandits for myself!"

And before the footman could get down to help her descend, the Dowager had stepped down from the coach and stood staring at Evan and Findlay. To his dismay, Evan found that he was perspiring and that his throat was growing tight. The Dowager tended to have that effect on people.

"Just give me your rings, ma'am!" he said in a deep voice, trying to look taller and wider than he was and adjusting the kerchief more firmly across his face. "Then no harm will come to you!"

Lady Barrisford sniffed. "What harm would come to me otherwise, young man?" she inquired. "I haven't the least intention of letting you have my jewelry. I've had it all my life, and I'm not giving it to some common thief just because he asks for it."

"I'm not a common thief!" exclaimed Evan indignantly. "I'm a highwayman! And you must give me your jewelry!"

"Then you come down here and get it, young man!" she said drily. "And if I don't wish to give it to you, I won't."

Reluctantly Evan swung down from his horse and approached her, extending his hand for the jewelry. As he did so, Lady Barrisford reached up and deftly wrenched the kerchief from his face.

"Evan Melville!" she exclaimed. "What on earth are you doing? Put that damned pistol down and get into this coach! And your friend, too!"

Evan did as he was told, but it proved quite unnecessary for young Findlay, for he had fainted at their first encounter and still lay sprawled in the dust.

"Well, we'll just sling him over his horse," said Evan heartlessly. "That'll get him home well enough."

By the time Lady Barrisford's hired postchaise had set her down at Merton Park, accompanied by Evan and the recumbent young Findlay, a settlement between the Dowager and the coachman had been reached so that there would be no reporting of the attempted robbery.

"Well, at least no one will be pressing charges against us," sighed Findlay in relief, having regained consciousness at last and listening to Evan's account of the latest developments.

"No, but I'm left without any money whatsoever because the Dowager wouldn't ante up. I'm afraid that I'll have to try another—"

"I don't believe you'll have to pay a penny, Evan, so put that out of your mind," interrupted Barrisford, who had been standing at the door of the library listening. "But you and I most certainly will be having a serious talk about gambling," he added.

Evan nodded, shamefaced. "When did you re

turn?" he asked. "I didn't think you were expected until next week."

"I wasn't. I'm here because I received an emergency message about you."

"From whom?" demanded Evan. "Oh, don't tell me. Thea has been spying again."

Barrisford shook his head. "David sent a message to your sister in London, and my grandmother notified me."

"David?" said Evan, astonished. "I didn't think he paid a bit of attention to anything that went on here."

"Well, he does," Barrisford assured him. "In fact, when I arrived here tonight, he was waiting to tell me where you had gone and that you had your pistols with you."

"He *told* you?" exclaimed Evan. "Do you mean he actually said it aloud?"

"Yes, he did," said Meredith, coming in with Thea and David. "He was afraid that you were about to get yourself killed—and you might have if you hadn't encountered Lady Barrisford."

Evan eyed his little brother for a moment. "Well, I don't appreciate being spied on, David—but at least you were trying to help." And he ruffled the boy's hair affectionately.

David moved closer to Barrisford and leaned against him slightly, and Meredith noted with some surprise that Barrisford put his arm lightly about the boy's shoulders and that David accepted it.

"It looks as though you're doing very well with everything here, Lord Barrisford," she said drily. "I can

see that my help is scarcely needed. Have you rea
Mr. Adams' letter yet?"

Barrisford nodded. "I need to talk to you abou
that privately," he said briskly, walking her to a sma
study across the passageway.

"Why do you need to speak to me privately?" sh
demanded. "The rest of the family will know abou
my engagement at once. Why not now?"

"Because you aren't going to marry Adams," h
responded. "I have sent him a letter refusing my pe
mission to the match."

"Lord Barrisford, you are overreaching yourself!
she exclaimed angrily. "I appreciate everything tha
you have done to help my family, but why are yo
interfering in a matter so nearly connected to m
happiness?"

"I intend to marry you myself," he remarked casu
ally, watching her face.

"And that is your proposal?" she gasped. "Just a
announcement that you intend to marry me, withou
asking me whether or not I wish it?"

"Well, I am, after all, your guardian," he remarke
unable to resist the temptation. "Who is to tell m
that I cannot?"

"I can tell you, Devlin, that you won't marry tha
girl against her will," remarked the Dowager, wh
had been listening at the door. "She has a home wit
me, and I believe that I can ask for guardianship unt
she is married."

The earl stared at his grandmother in consterna
tion. "The devil you say! You know that I was teasin
her when I said that she had no choice!"

The Dowager stared at him with no trace of a smile.
I may know it, but I am less certain that she does.
And I am less certain still that you don't still feel that
you have the upper hand and glory in it."

Turning to Meredith, she said, "I can guarantee
you my protection and an income that will keep you
the rest of your life, so that you may choose whom
you marry and indeed whether or not you marry at
all, my dear. Will you come with me?"

Meredith looked from her to the astonished Barrisford and nodded. "I will get my things," she said.
It's clear that Lord Barrisford can take care of my
family, so I need have no worry there."

"You mean that you'll just walk away from us?" demanded Barrisford angrily.

"Why should I not?" she inquired coolly.

"Because you love Anthea and your brothers!"

"Of course I do—but they are taken care of, aren't
they?"

He struggled with himself for a moment, then said,
"Then stay for me, Merry—because I need you and
because I ask you to. If you don't wish to marry me,
of course you don't have to do so—but stay with us."

Meredith walked over to him and looked up at him.
"Do you love me, sir?" she asked abruptly.

He stared down at her for a moment, then pulled
her into his arms. "Yes," he murmured into her ear.
"Yes, yes, I do."

"What was that, Devlin?" called the interested
Dowager, who was surrounded now by the rest of the
family.

After a moment Barrisford looked up and grinned.

"I said 'yes,' you devil—just as you knew I would."
Turning back to Meredith, he whispered, "Will you
marry me now, my dear?"

And she nodded as he folded her into his arms
again.

"Speak up, Devlin!" demanded his grandmother.
"We can't hear you properly!"

Lord Barrisford walked to the door and firmly
closed it in the faces of the assembled group. Then
gathering Meredith in his arms, he started once more
to kiss her, but she held up her hand to stop him.

"What's wrong?" he asked. "Have you changed
your mind already, Miss Melville?"

"Perhaps," she responded, smiling up at him. "Do
you remember Mrs. Danvers?" she inquired.

"There's no need to talk about her—" he began,
but she put her finger to his lips.

"Do you remember her?" she repeated.

He nodded reluctantly.

"And do you remember the vase that I cracked
across your head, my dear?"

He grinned and pointed to the small scar. "I believe so, ma'am, if the blow has not unhinged my
faculties."

"And do you make the connection, sir?" she asked.

He looked down at her in consternation, his brow
knit. "Are you threatening me with physical violence,
Miss Melville?" he inquired.

She shook her head. "I am merely pointing out
that hearts break quite as easily as heads and vases,
sir. And I don't wish for breakage of any of the three."

"I am relieved to hear it," he murmured, pulling

her close once more, "for that means there will be none."

And for the first time in what seemed like a lifetime, Merry knew that she had come home.

Epilogue

"Open the door wider, Jenkins! We're bringing in the Yule log!" shouted Barrisford, as he and David and Evan struggled with the massive log they had selected from the nearby woods. Together the three of them stumbled into the Hall and managed to place it on the stone hearth.

There was a general shout as the rest of the family crowded around the hearth and admired their choice.

"Who should light it?" asked Barrisford, looking around the group.

"David," answered Evan. "He's the one who kept it going last year in London."

"So he did," agreed Barrisford, looking down at the boy with affection. "What made you so interested in that log, David?"

David paused a moment. "It's us," he said in a low voice. He talked now, but more slowly and in a softer voice than he had before.

"What do you mean, 'it's us'?" asked Evan.

"It's the family," explained David. "I thought that as long as I could keep the fire going, the family would stay together. When it stopped, we went away to Merton Park and left Merry."

"But you didn't leave me for long, my dear," responded his sister. "I was there very soon." She looked around the group gathered at the fire. "And now we're all here."

David nodded and smiled, leaning forward to light the fire. "A Merry Christmas to everyone!" he called, as it caught fire.

"A Merry Christmas!" echoed the others.

"Well, I have my Christmas wish," said the Dowager, smiling.

"What was it?" demanded Thea.

"Don't you remember?" said the Dowager. "Last Christmas in London I wished that I would see Devlin settled at Sutherland with his family—and here we are."

She looked down affectionately at the cradle close to her feet and at her grandson standing with his arm around Merry. Evan and Thea leaned against one another and David sat close to the cradle, three dogs curled close beside him.

"Are you sorry we're not at Merton Park?" Barrisford whispered into his wife's ear.

"No," she said simply, looking happily around the room and then into his eyes. "Home is where you are."

Then she could hear the voices of Thea and Evan, raised together in song.

Now unto my lady
Promise to her I make,
From all others only
To her I me betake.

ABOUT THE AUTHOR

Mona Gedney lives with her family in West Lafayette, IN. She is the author of nine Zebra Regency romances. Mona loves to hear from readers, and you may write to her c/o Zebra Books. Please include a self-addressed stamped envelope if you wish a response.

BOOK YOUR PLACE ON OUR WEBSITE AND MAKE THE READING CONNECTION!

We've created a customized website just for our very special readers, where you can get the inside scoop on everything that's going on with Zebra, Pinnacle and Kensington books.

When you come online, you'll have the exciting opportunity to:

- View covers of upcoming books

- Read sample chapters

- Learn about our future publishing schedule (listed by publication month *and author*)

- Find out when your favorite authors will be visiting a city near you

- Search for and order backlist books from our online catalog

- Check out author bios and background information

- Send e-mail to your favorite authors

- Meet the Kensington staff online

- Join us in weekly chats with authors, readers and other guests

- Get writing guidelines

- AND MUCH MORE!

Visit our website at
http://www.zebrabooks.com

ROMANCE FROM JANELLE TAYLOR

ANYTHING FOR LOVE   (0-8217-4992-7, $5.99)

DESTINY MINE   (0-8217-5185-9, $5.99)

CHASE THE WIND   (0-8217-4740-1, $5.99)

MIDNIGHT SECRETS   (0-8217-5280-4, $5.99)

MOONBEAMS AND MAGIC   (0-8217-0184-4, $5.99)

SWEET SAVAGE HEART   (0-8217-5276-6, $5.99)

ROMANCE FROM FERN MICHAELS

DEAR EMILY   (0-8217-4952-8, $5.99)

WISH LIST   (0-8217-5228-6, $6.99)

AND IN HARDCOVER:

VEGAS RICH   (1-57566-057-1, $25.00)